THE STONEHENGE SCRIBBLES

An Hystorical Fantasie

from

Jamie Jenkyn

The works of Jamie Jenkyn

Through dedicated and assiduous exploration and research, author Jamie Jenkyn has unearthed previously untold stories from our history You may think that the great events of the British past, from the Iron Age to the present Information Age, just had to happen. Not so!! A missed encounter here, a wrong word there, and all could have been different. If roving royal eyes had fallen on other damsels, if steely soldierly swords had swung in an infinitesimally different fashion, if lumbering horses had (or had not) stumbled as they rushed into battle, our present would not be what it is today. It has been Jenkyn's life's work (at least for the past couple of years), to root out these fortunate (or unfortunate) situations that had historic implications, so that all may know how tenuous our path to where we are really was.

With ultimate respect for known facts and a haughty disregard for speculation (unless such an approach gets in the way of a good joke) Jenkyn demonstrates how close we came to having a country that would not have been as wonderful (or as terrible) as the one we currently enjoy.

Do not miss any of the delightful and informative little books in this series.

But one word of warning - read at your own risk, you may die laughing.

INTRODUCTORY NOTE

If you don't think about it very much, or you haven't studied too much history, you probably think that your country has been here since the beginning of time, constant and unchanging. Forever England, past and present, and all that. Not so, my friend. Of course, you'll probably know that the USA is a recent construction, created by European robbers helping themselves to other people's land and then dumping the greedy monarchies that funded their activities. But you will undoubtedly dismiss the USA as a temporary aberration in the grand scheme of things and not really worth bothering about anyway. And, should you be one of those rare creatures who have investigated the past more assiduously, you might also know that what we now call Germany and Italy were cobbled together from collections of small, insignificant and disparate entities who had previously spent their energies in quarrelling with each other. But, as you know, the real world begins somewhere around Bristol and ends abruptly at Dover, so the machinations of continental codgers have nothing to do with anything. No, you believe, England is as it always was, except for those insignificant appendages of Scotland, Wales and Ireland that your ancestors kindly allowed to attach themselves to your great nation.

Amazingly, this is a distorted view of the existence of the world's leading and most important geopolitical conglomeration. When God created the world, he did not create England and then those other inconsequential bits. No sir, the rest of the planet Earth is not the spare rib of King Arthur and Queen Boudicca's great realm. You will be surprised to know that, unbelievably, England was formed by fire and sword just like everywhere else. Sadly banal, but there it is. And indeed, had it not been for certain events which occurred many centuries ago, your much-loved homeland would not now 'be'. If fortune had flowed in a slightly different direction, your green and pleasant land could now be known as Scotland, or Ireland, or even, heaven forbid, France.

As a disinterested observer, it seems to me an inequitable situation that you should remain in ignorance of your heritage, for it is a truism that knowledge of the past secures the future. Hence, in this little volume, I have resolved to write down an account of these momentous events to which I have eluded above. Read on, sir (or madam) and be prepared to be surprised and illuminated.

Francis Phibba

Historian and Author

1. A LOAD OF KOBBLERS

Before I plunge head first into the narrative of these important historical occurrences, it is incumbent upon me to make some reference to the source of my information. Indeed, were I not to so do, I would risk being dismissed as a charlatan and lacking in academic rigour, so you will excuse my little diversion from the main thrust in the interests of historical credibility.

My researches were inspired by a discovery I made one day on a walking expedition with my good friend Joanie in the wilds of Wiltshire. (By the way, Joanie was a wonderful companion and I miss her so much, but she unfortunately fell victim to the Curse. But more of that later. For now, let us concentrate on the evidence.)

In the heart of this venerable county where I spent so many happy hours with my now departed friend, there can be found an ancient monument of some historical, and indeed religious, significance. This crude edifice is much beloved by certain ladies and gentlemen who are attracted to celebrate there in ragged clothes, at times when they judge the movement of the heavens to be in propitious positions. It was not here at Stonehenge I made my discovery; but nearby is a site where the constructors of the famous stone circle are said to have rested and taken refreshment (or so many distinguished archaeologists tell us, and who am I to challenge them?) While Joanie and I were stumbling around near this location, I came across a collection of small stones with marks scratched on them. I gave them the name Stonehenge Stones, and they revealed wondrous previously unknown facts to me. Once I started to decipher the meanings of the marks, the essence of the tale I now tell was laid before me.

Ah, you say, hold on! What learning was given to you that you were able to understand such an early form of writing, previously unknown to anyone? Well, I have *extensive experience in coding and ciphers. And you also may be comforted by the fact that these Stones are now in the hands of a celebrated museum, and when the illustrious antiquarians catch up with my thinking, they will undoubtedly confirm my translation. When that happens, the facts that I now lay before you will be truly indisputable in all reputable academic circles.*

The documents were dated, but using but using a system of counting which is now lost to history. However, certain technological references contained in the Stones lead to the conclusion that the action takes place during the Iron Age, in a period that predates the arrival of the advanced equipment that the Romans brought with them when they invaded your cherished soil.

You can see the efforts I have gone to in the interest of historical accuracy, but one final word of warning. As always in these matters, the information contained in the source documents is always incomplete, and to render the content intelligible there is a need to resort to making things up, or, as the archaeologist and historians call it, 'deduction'. However, you can be sure that the deductions I have had to make are likely to be much less controversial than the current arguments that rage over so much of history, even very recent history. So, dear sir (or madam), read on with confidence and plunge into the wild tale of turbulent past times from which your heritage surfaced...

The scribbles on the Stonehenge Stones tell us of two great families. The first of these, the Headmans, were the dominant family in the lands of which these Stones speak. They were, if you like, the head of their tribe. The other family were at the absolute bottom of the hierarchy, for indeed even in those times a flourishing class system dictated an individual's place in society. This lowly family were the Kobblers, and were, quite appropriately, at the foot of the pile. But the Kobblers had many assets denied to the more elevated Headmans. For a start, they were infinitely more useful to the people of the time than the Headmans. While virile healthy citizens of the period could easily survive without recourse to headgear, all of them were totally reliant on having at least one good, sturdy pair of boots. And as the Hunters, the Farmers, the Herders, the Armours and the rest trundled back from their nearest Kobbler's roundhouse with their new footwear, they would mumble among themselves.

"Bloody good pair of boots these, mate"

"Dunno what we'd do without 'em Kobblers, eh?"

"Too true, me old clay beaker, them be a real asset."

"Yeah, unlike them Headmans. More like assholes than assets, they be."

"They bleedin' well are, and too full of themselves, if you ask me."

So you can see that discontent and insurrection was already in the air. But the Kobblers had another asset. Because their services were so in demand, they had the wherewithal to support larger families. So, unlike the Headmans, the Kobblers were ubiquitous. Everywhere you looked in these Iron Age encampments, you saw crowds of little Kobblers running around with their makeshift swords and toy shields, shouting "to battle, to battle," although they had no idea what exactly that meant. There were so many of them that you had to keep your wits about you to avoid stepping on one, for if you did, you risked the whole extended family descending on you seeking revenge.

The Headmans were well aware how extensively the Kobblers outnumbered them, and it was a situation they could not allow to continue. Various schemes were tried to limit the numbers of their adversaries. The Headmans despatched young Kobblers, with their toy weapons in their hands, out to defend the community, but the Armours, who were the traditional militia of the tribe, took offence at being usurped and sent them back before any harm could come to them. A limit on the extent of procreation was tried, but the people of the time were a randy lot and would not stand for such impositions on fundamental liberties.

Faced with this uncontrolled infestation of Kobblers, the Headmans reverted to schemes to increase their own numbers. However, they were smart enough to realise that there was little point in producing shedloads of kids if they couldn't afford to feed them. Then they came up with the idea of stealing a little bit off everyone else in the community, so they would have enough to nourish their much needed offspring. They called this innovation 'taxation', but it proved to be a totally unpopular idea. Nevertheless, even in the face of loud protest they went ahead with it anyway, thereby turning the whole community against them.

And so it was, as the Stones tell us, that the conditions were set for a great revolution that would turn society on its head and lead to a new order that would herald the beginnings of what would become the greatest kingdom in the known, and indeed unknown, world. But how exactly did these changes come about? Read on, sir (or madam) and all will be made clear.

2. THE BIRTH OF THE GREAT ONE

On deciphering the scratchings on the Stones, I learned that the arrival in this world of a newborn Headman was an occasion of great joy and celebration – for the Headmans. The other families in the settlement turned away and got on with their daily business. It had been suggested in times gone by that if they were to incentivise the whole community to join in the festivities for the new baby, it would help instil loyalty among the tribe when the new arrival became their leader. But the Headmans weren't the sort of people to put their hands in their pockets for such vague promises. So instead they invited their own relatives from the surrounding subservient encampments to wet the baby's head, at their invitees' own expense, of course. Motivated by both family obligation and fear of reprisals if they did not show face, the guests all turned up and the new-born was thus greeted by a modest but adequate gathering of admirers.

The tone of the writing in the Stones does hint strongly at these sort of festivities being the normal course of events, but, in any case, whether this celebration was a one-off or a regular rite is not material to the import of the tale I am in the process of relating. For, as you will see, the repercussions of this birth were to stretch well beyond the narrow confines of one family, or one settlement, or, indeed, one small conglomeration of roundhouse villages.

The Headman baby mentioned in the Stones was a boy, and we are told his father was Bowleg Headman. Bowleg was a nickname, an account of the shape of his lower limbs. His given name was Bob, and he liked to be known as Chieftain Bob, for he was the senior member of the family and hence the ruler of all the citizens of not only his own encampment, but of several others close by. Yes indeed, Bowleg was a man of note in the community, and he held the reins of power, although somewhat more tenuously than he realised.

For those of you with an interest in social history, it behoves me to point out that knowledge of paternity was not widespread at the time in this part of Britain.

The ladies of the settlements were very free with their favours, and, to be blunt, if they fancied doing it with any passing male, they did. Children took their mother's names, for who knew who their fathers were? The offspring joined the family creche, where they were looked after by the older female members of the family.

The Headmans, however, scorned this practice. As the ruling group, they were obsessed by the purity of their blood, and refused to mate with anyone outside of their extended family, and not too extended at that. If you know anything of the Spanish Hapsburg dynasty, you will be aware that such intensive inbreeding has disastrous results. But this was not well understood in prehistoric times, and the prevalence of physical and mental disorders in the Headmans was put down to sheer bad luck, or perhaps the stress of wielding power. And it is to be noted that the latest Headman baby, the son and heir of Bowleg, did not escape from this misfortune. So the sad story of the young Bo' Ring Headman being dogged by ill fortune had it's beginnings right at the start of his life.

By a strange coincidence, another baby was brought into the world that very same day. *Let me say that this may be more legend than fact, for in the Stones the story of this baby was written after the event, and may have been embellished to add to the aura that came to surround this new arrival.* It appears that the celebrations for this birth were even more boisterous than those for the young Bo' Ring, for he was a Kobbler, and as you have already learned, the Kobblers were thick on the ground and financially comfortable, and it was much to the annoyance of Bowleg that his celebrations were being put in the shade by the party of these upstarts.

Even as a newly born baby, Thomakin Kobbler was an exceptional personage. His mother had been smitten by love and the idea of fidelity, and so everyone knew who his father was. Thomakin was the son of a handsome, sturdy and skilful member of the Armour family, and this meant that not only was he blessed by having numerous relatives of both lineages who would always be faithful to him, he had dexterity with both the sword and the hammer flowing in his veins, and those were attributes that would stand him in good stead when he was called upon to play his part in history.

3. THE GREAT ONE'S CHILDHOOD

The Stones not only recount that two central protagonists in this great world-changing episode of history were born in the same little encampment, but it also confirms that, in that very place, they developed from children into boys, and from boys into young men. And yet, location was the only feature that was common to their upbringings.

For reasons already explained, Bo' Ring was a sickly little baby and he grew up into a weedy waif of a boy, constantly affected by various afflictions and illnesses, and the Herbalist and the Druid were constant visitors to the Headman roundhouse. The state of his health constantly worried his mother and irritated his father.

"Aaarh, I fear the boy will not survive to succeed you, Bowleg," the mother would say.

"Desist in your idle speculation, woman. He'll get over all this. And don't call me Bowleg, my name's Bob, Chieftain Bob even," her husband would reply.

"OK Bowleg," she would answer, and old Bowleg would treat her to slap around the ear. *(This was an era before women's rights were universally recognised)*

"Put the boy outside and let him get a bit of fresh air. Do him the world of good," the village chieftain would command.

"But Bow… Bob, it's cold and it's raining."

"It's always cold and raining. Chuck him out!"

"Well, at least let me put a hat on 'im."

"Oh, if you must. But only because it's an advertisement for the family firm."

And so the young Bo' Ring would be seen wandering around the settlement, wrapped up in several layers of smocks and capes, his little hat on his head, with his mother always hanging around in the background, ready to pick him up at the slightest sign of a fall or a stumble. The poor boy always played alone, for his mother was terrified he would catch some deadly disease from the other riff-raff children. Her fears were unfounded, because in no circumstances would they have played with him anyway. They were forbidden on pain of death to have any contact with him, on account of the fact his father had taken advantage of his birth to increase the taxes, on the pretence that he needed more support for his growing family.

The childhood of Thomakin Kobbler was a complete contrast, so the Stones tell us. It is recorded there that the boy Thomakin had been the most popular young lad in the settlement. As you have already learned, he was unique in that his links to two families were known, while all the other kids could only claim connection to one. Such an advantage could have instilled jealousy among his contemporaries, but Thomakin was apparently of such a sweet, helpful and loving nature that the boys followed him around and imitated his every action. As for the girls, they would swoon if he even cast a sideways glance in their direction. Previously, the great families of the encampment pretty well kept themselves to themselves, but the existence of the young Kobbler began to draw them together.

The boy was accepted easily into both the Kobbler and the Armour families, especially after his father was killed in a skirmish while defending the community. His mother refused all other advances and died soon after from grief. Sympathy for the little orphan drew the people of the encampment together, not only the Kobblers and the Armours, but the Farmers, the Herders, the Stitchers and all the others, with the exception of the Headmans, of course. It may seem strange to us modern historians, but the Headmans missed the implications for their rule of this social change, and continue to bump up their unpopular taxes willy-nilly, and in other ways oppress the populace with their self-serving greed and utter contempt for others.

The chroniclers single out one key encounter between Bo' Ring and Thomakin, and as this is significant in our story, I will recount it to you now. It happened one day when they were both about ten years old. Bo' Ring was ambling around the settlement on his own, as usual. His Mother no longer followed him around, as she had continued to procreate assiduously, and the boy's numerous siblings now occupied her time. Unusually, Thomakin too happened to be on his own and the two boys came across each other a few yards from the main Kobbler residence.

"Hey, Headman, you stupid cripple, why don't you bugger off back to your own bit," young Kobbler shouted. His amiable kindness towards others did not extend to the hated Headmans.

Bo' Ring, who wasn't used to the riff-raff addressing him, took a few seconds to reply. "Listen you, we are the rulers here, and the whole village belongs to us. It's time you learned your place. Down on your knees and beg forgiveness from your master."

"An' what'll you do if I don't?" Thomakin sneered.

"I'll make you." And, so saying, Bo' Ring raised his fists and took a step towards his adversary.

"Don't make me laugh, you insipid insect."

This reply had the effect of infuriating the Headman boy; he took another step to within contact range and swung his arm violently. He missed.

Thomakin, still laughing, pushed him to the ground. "Run off back home, mummy's boy, before I lose my temper and do something I regret."

Whimpering, Bo' Ring raised himself from the ground and scuttled back the more affluent end of the settlement, leaving a trail of tears in his wake.

If that had been all that had happened, the incident would have been of no consequence. But, unknown to both Bo' Ring and Thomakin, the altercation had been observed by a third party. Concealed behind a nearby roundhouse, Beaufox, the second of the Headman sprogs and next in line to the chieftainship after Bo' Ring, had witnessed the total humiliation of his big brother. It made him furious. Who was this boy who had so shamed the heir to the Headman dynasty? This could not be allowed to stand. The family honour demanded revenge, and he, Beaufox, would see that it was obtained.

Now, physically, the younger Headman was as much a weedy and insignificant being as his elder brother, but there was one clear difference between them. Beaufox was not half as stupid as Bo' Ring; in fact he was a devious and cunning little runt who would stoop to anything to achieve his ends.

Although Thomakin Kobbler did not know it, that day he had made a formidable enemy. He would live to regret it.

4.CLASS WAR

When he reached the age of fourteen, Thomakin Kobbler was faced with a decision of ominous import. It was a unique choice, for, if the Stones are to be believed, he was the first youth in the history of British social history to have to face it. Previously, if you were born into the Farmer family, your name was Farmer and you farmed; if you were born into the Hunter family you were called Hunter and you hunted; if you were born into the Herder family, you were known as Herder and you herded cows and sheep. It was, and ever had been, the traditional way.

Now sir (or madam), please do not jump to the conclusion that the young Kobbler was of an iconoclastic disposition and took delight in overthrowing traditions. If anything, the opposite was the case, at least at this point in his life. But, as you have seen, Thomakin was special in that he knew who BOTH his mother and father had been, and he therefore had a foot in two family camps, as it were. On his mother's side, he was a Kobbler, and indeed he had taken this name. In the normal scheme of things, he would grow up to craft boots and shoes. But his father had been an Armour, and the calling of this family dictated that he should pursue a military career. But which of the two paths was it to be? Was he to make war or make footwear? In the end, Thomakin decided to remain faithful to the ancient rules and apply himself to the hammer and the last.

Before he made this decisive choice, Thomakin had of course helped in the Kobbler family business by carrying out various menial tasks, like brushing the floor and cleaning the hides ready for use. But this didn't take up all his free time, and he had taken the opportunity to develop the skill of his other family. In fact, for his age, he was the best spear carrier and swordsman in the settlement, and the Armours' felt his loss keenly when he opted for a shoemaking career. And not only had he found time for the Armours, but such was his popularity that he had been allowed to spend some time with the Hunters, and had also developed prodigious prowess with a bow and arrow.

Thomakin devoted himself to his shoemaking career. Within a few years he had become a master craftsman, who specialised in the creation of the sturdy and ornate boots used in battle or on great ceremonial occasions. Indeed, as you would expect of someone with so many multi-faceted talents, he was the go-to source for all such footwear. However, he still managed to find a little time to pursue his previous interests. He was so endowed that, in spite of the limited time he had to devote to these activities, the whole encampment recognised him as the outstanding warrior of the village, unmatched in the skills of both archery and hand-to- hand combat. The whole encampment, that is, with the exception of the Headmans. They were of the kind who favoured propaganda over truth, to the extent that they could hardly see their hands in front of their faces. In the opinion of Bowleg Bowman, the great fighters of the village, after the leader himself of course, were his two frail and weedy sons, Bo' Ring and Beaufox.

In one section of the palaeolithic-style tablets that recount this story, under the heading Significant Crimes, I found a report that details a very significant event concerning Thomakin and the Headmans. This record allowed me to recreate the events that I describe below.

In accordance with the customs of the settlement, when the eldest son of a chieftain reaches the age of eighteen years old, he is accorded a coming-of-age ceremony in which he is designated as his father's heir. Chief Bowleg, his finances boosted by the unfair taxes he was extorting from his subjects, resolved that his son would have the most prestigious celebration that the encampment had ever known. The Stitchers were commanded to make great robes for all the Headmans, and the ruling family itself undertook the preparation of elaborate ceremonial helmets. But the centrepiece of any ritual costume were the boots, which had to be such garishly decorated footwear that all the other items would seem dull in comparison. No matter how imposing the helmet, how magnificent the cloak, wear a shoddy pair of boots and you were branded forever as a nobody. The boots had to be made by the best, and when the order for two pairs one for Bo' Ring and another for Beaufox, was transmitted to the Kobblers, the task was naturally assigned to young Thomakin.

Two days before the festivities, Thomakin ambled up to the chieftain's roundhouse, two pairs of well-crafted ornate boots under his arm. When he arrived at the door, he shouted out, "Bo' Ring, get yourself out here. I've come wif your boots."

Bo' Ring rushed to the entrance with a beam of expectation on is face, but this turned to a scowl when he saw who had brought the footwear. He had assiduously avoided this particular Kobbler since that day, eight years earlier, when he had been so utterly humiliated by him. And he certainly was not going to risk being accosted by the fiend again. He silently turned his back and went inside, empty handed.

Thomakin stood there, a tad upset, as he had spent may hours on these boots and he intended to be paid for them, one way or the other. But a minute later the younger brother, Beaufox, came out of the hut and, in a sneering voice, spoke to the waiting Kobbler. "My brother can't stand the sight of you, Kobbler. If it wasn't for the importance of the ceremony, and the desire of my father for it to be perfect, we'd send you back to your grubby hole along with your manky footwear. But we'll take them, against our better judgement. Hand them over!"

Thomakin frowned at him, and held out an open palm. "Payment first, then boots."

"You insolent serf, we decide when you will receive payment."

The Kobbler shrugged his shoulders and turned his back.

"All right. All right!" screamed Beaufox, "Here's your bloody coins. These boots just better be up to scratch."

Thomakin left, smiling and weighing the money in his hand, and Beaufox turned about and carried both pairs of boots into the roundhouse.

Now sir (or madam), what happened next is not recorded in the account of the criminal trial which followed, and the facts did not come to light until the wily Beaufox confessed on his deathbed to one of the anonymous etchers of the stones. I include here, slightly out of sequence, because its knowledge is essential to a full understanding of the events. Such is the work of a serious historical researcher.

As Beaufox entered the gloomy surroundings of the family's living space, he inspected both pairs of boots carefully, making sure he could identify which were his brother's (the larger ones) and which were his own. Then Beaufox surreptitiously hid the larger pair in his own corner of the living area before handing the smaller pair to his big brother.

Now, some of you may not know this, but while wearing a pair of boots too large for you can sometimes be uncomfortable, wearing a pair a couple of sizes too small is always excruciatingly painful. And although this may not be known to you, sir (or madam), you can be assured it was well-known to the wily young Beaufox Headman - and indeed it was a key part of his plan.

5. TOO BIG FOR HIS BOOTS

As was the custom, Bo' Ring Headman did not touch any of his ceremonial costume until the just before his coming-of-age event. Tradition demanded he did not get dressed up until the great occasion was about to commence. At the appointed hour, he began by putting on the tunic and the sumptuously decorated great cloak, and when he looked down at himself, he was delighted. Attire worthy of a great Chieftain, or a King-to-be. The helmet came next, fashioned by his own family, and splendidly encrusted with jewels they had acquired in a more or less legitimate fashion from a passing merchant.

"What do you think, Beaufox?" he asked his brother.

"Magnificent. Old Uncle Bo-Tox has done you proud."

"Yes, indeed he has. And now for the pièce de resistance." So saying, Bo' Ring bent down and picked up the boots Thomakin had made. "Beautifully fashioned, I have to admit, even though I detest the scoundrel who made them." He bent over and pulled them on, not without some difficulty. His face reddened and his features twisted in an agony. He could have been in the process of being possessed by a demon, but his younger brother knew better.

"Problem?" Beaufox asked, sweetly.

"They're... too... damned...tight," his brother gasped. "Get Daddy... Now."

"Right," Beaufox said, and as he turned his face away a broad grin lit up his countenance. He was still beaming as he left in search of his father.

Bo' Ring wrestled the boots off and threw them angrily the ground, and when Beaufox returned with Bowleg and the Druid, the heir was standing there bare-footed, rubbing his toes.

His father was not happy. "What are you playing at, Bo' Ring, you should be ready for the ceremony. Cathbad here has consulted the runes and today the auspices are propitious, are they not, Druid?"

"Indeed they are, your excellence. The young man whom we welcome to manhood today will have destiny at this feet."

"But not at his bare feet," Beaufox said, stifling a giggle

"No indeed, get your boots on immediately, young sir. Our whole family and guests are ready and waiting. Let us have no more delay," the father commanded.

"But father, I can't wear therm. They hurt my feet. They're too small," Bo' Ring whimpered.

"Don't be a baby. Get the boots on."

Bo' Ring made another attempt to insert his feet into the footwear but it was too much. He collapsed onto the ground and kicked them off, writhing.

"Are your boots OK, Beaufox?" the father asked.

"Oh, very comfortable," the younger brother simpered.

"Then this is an outrage. Which of those useless Kobblers made those boots for my most important son?"

Beaufox was quick to provide the required information. "The young Thomakin Kobbler, father."

"What a useless idiot. He's fit for nothing," Bowleg raged.

"But father, if I may suggest, that is not true. Indeed, he has an excellent reputation in the encampment as the best bootmaker anyone can remember. I think there may be darker forces at work here." Beaufox's face adopted a mien of evil intrigue.

"Darker forces! Darker forces!! Do you know anything about this, Cathbad?"

The Druid trembled and shook his head.

"If I may be allowed to explain, father. You see, Thomakin Kobbler doesn't like Bo' Ring, he has never liked him, and I fear it may have been his intention to…" Beaufox paused to let his father come to the obvious conclusion.

"To what, you idiot?" Bowleg bellowed. "What kind of son of mine cannot finish his sentences?"

"To…you know…sabotage…"

"Sabotage what? By the runes, you don't mean that this Kobbler was out to ruin my son's ceremony?"

Beaufox shrugged, as if he too found the suggestion almost unbelievable.

"Fetch the rogue! Send the Armours out to bring the fiend to me. I'll cut his bloody throat."

"I'll see to it, Dad." And the triumphant Beaufox left at a fast trot.

Cathbad the Druid sidled up to Bowleg and whispered in a tone that suggested an apology for interrupting the thoughts of the great man. "My Lord, I really don't think you should assassinate the young man."

"Not assassinate him. By the gods, priest, not only will I kill him, but I'll cut him into little pieces and hang them up all over the encampment as a lesson to anyone who thinks they can treat the Headmans with anything less than respect."

Cathbad coughed, "Err… Bad idea."

"What are you talking about? Why is it a bad idea?"

"Two reasons, my Lord. First of all, there are processes to be followed if you don't want to incite the wrath of the gods. He will have to be accused and judged in a trial presided over by a Druid priest. Only if found guilty can he be punished."

"No problem, Cathbad. I'll accuse him, you'll judge him and pronounce him guilty, then I'll get my knife out."

"Well, I wouldn't actually kill him, my Lord. You see, he is very well-liked throughout the settlement and if you did away with him just because he made a pair of boots a bit too small, it wouldn't go down well. You wouldn't want your subjects to rise up against you?"

"They wouldn't dare. The Armours would take care of them if they did."

"Possibly, but..."

"But what? Protecting my interests, that's their job."

"Well...technically, no. Their job, according to the will of the gods, is to protect the community. And, you see, this

Thomakin Kobbler is a particular favourite of the Armours, on account of his father."

"He know his father? Impossible, these degenerate women sleep with a different man every night."

"Not Thomakin's mother. She only had the one lover: one of the Armours. Of course, it's your decision. Kill him if you want, but if I were you I wouldn't risk it. But I have a suggestion. We can find the boy guilty, and you can then banish him from the community. The Armours won't like it, but they will accept it, if I tell them that the gods wish it."

The writing on the Stones tell us this is what they did, but it was an unsatisfactory solution for everyone involved. Thomakin was naturally upset about haven to leave the only home he had ever known, and his families and friends were very distressed to see him go. There were some young ladies who were particularly miffed, for they were enamoured of the young Kobbler and had frequently offered him their charms. But he had declined, saying that he had vowed to emulate his parents and find one true love to whom he would be forever faithful. The more persistent among his admirers had similarly decided to protect their purity, in the hope they would be the chosen one, and were now regretting all the fun they had missed.

Those on the Headman side were similarly disappointed. Bowleg was beside himself for having his wishes thwarted, and in addition to finding that he had incurred an obligation to the Druid, Cathbad. Cathbad himself worried that he had been forced to provide his ruler with unwelcome advice. Young Bo' Ring was mortified that he had revealed his true worthless wimpish character to his father. Even Beaufox, who seemed to have got what he wanted, felt thwarted in his real ambition to have the scum Thomakin Kobbler removed permanently from the face of the earth. It was an event that left scars everywhere, and all of these scars would fester as events progressed.

Millenia later, even now the event is having repercussions. As I write this, my tears flow in memory of my dear departed Joanie. When I had just translated the part of the story, I recounted it to her. Quite naturally and justifiably, she was furious at the antics of Beaufox Headman, but just as angry at the Druid,

Cathbad. Even my explanation that the prehistoric cleric had saved Thomakin's life did nothing to quell her wrath. If only she had listened to my advice. My friends, I advise you never to get on the wrong side of a Druid. That's all I'm saying.

6. THE BANISHMENT

The Stonehenge Stones only provide very sketchy details of Thomakin Kobbler's life in the period immediately following his banishment from the settlement of his birth. When he eventually returned, he was on the way to the apogee of his advancement and the chroniclers drooled over every aspect of his life, but before that very little was written. Joanie and I gleaned from the subsequent events of Thomakin's story that this unrecorded period of his life must have been traumatic and influential, for the man who returned was completely different from the boy who had left. "We need to find out more about his exile," I said to my friend and she agreed.

We understood that we had taken on an impossible task. In England, the period in which Thomakin lived was pre-history; there was no written record. Our etched Stones were an exception. What were the chances of us stumbling upon another hoard like them?

And even if we did, how likely was it that they would contain further details of the life and times of Thomakin Kobbler. The odds were astronomic. But all was not quite lost. The Stonehenge scribblings gave us two clues. Firstly, they told us that the banished peasant had headed off in a southerly direction, which would have taken him towards the coast. And they also mentioned that Thomakin had spent some time across the seas, in a land we now call Europe but at that time was known to the population only as 'somewhere else'.

Then Joanie pointed out that while England was stuck in pre-history, Europe was teeming with Romans who had a surfeit of generals, writers and historians all furiously recording everything that was going on. I knew then where we had to go. Rome. A few months of scouring around in the archives of Republican Rome in the Antiquity Centre there would yield up some valuable info on our hero, if we were lucky. And we were indeed lucky.

The great Roman historian Livy (or one of his minions) wrote of a gentleman called Tomacus Britannicus, or Tomacus Sutor, which means Thomas the Shoemaker, so we can be pretty certain he was talking about our Thomakin. The facts contained in these Roman ramblings are not entirely dependable, as Livy was known as a bit of a propagandist, but I will recount them anyway and leave you to make up your own minds.

As soon as the verdict was pronounced, Thomakin was taken from his trial with nothing but the clothes he was wearing. An iron collar was placed around his neck, and he was led by a chain to the farthest perimeter of Bowleg's domain, surrounded by a group of the Armours and accompanied by the Druid. Thomakin was overtaken by sorrow at the apparent betrayal of his father's family, a feeling intensified by seeing one of his kinsmen bearing his shield and carrying his weapons. I've not yet gone and already they're stealing my stuff, he thought.

Cathbad the Druid commanded them to stop at a clearing in the middle of the forest. "This is the limit of Lord

Bowleg's power. Beyond here, other chieftains reign, with the permission and support of the gods and we priests. Let this faithless cur be banished, and let him take his chances with whatever fate has in store for him."

One of the Armours removed the iron collar from Thomakin's neck, and he stepped away.

"Hold him, there are further rituals that have to be observed," Cathbad ordered.

The Armours ignored him. The soldier carrying his weapons handed them over to the impeding exile. Then Thomakin's uncle, the half-brother of his dead father, began whispering to his nephew. "It's a bloody shame it's come to this, lad, but what can we do? Them in power have got their rules; you made a mistake and you have to pay for it."

"I be innocent, Uncle. Them boots I made were the perfect size. Someone's been up to mischief to get rid of me out of our village. Them Headmans be afeard of me."

"I believe you, son, but they be holding all the cards."

"Whether they be or not, Uncle, I will have my revenge. I swear it on my dead parents' souls."

Cathbad, who had not noticed this conversation going as he was diverted by preparing himself for some great ritual, suddenly became aware of it. "Desist," he squealed. "What are you two talking about?"

"Can a brave soldier not say farewell to his kinsman?"

The Druid pulled himself up to his full height, which wasn't very high. Then realising he was dwarfed by the surrounding Armours, raised his staff above his head and waved it around imperiously. His confidence fortified, he cried out, "Who gave this man those arms? Take them from him, now."

The Uncle took a step towards the priest and pulled his sword from his sheath. "We Amours will not allow one of ours to go forth into the wilderness unarmed. The weapons stay with him."

The Druid took a step back to comparative safety. "Well, OK then. But he is to have the Curse put upon him. It is the custom and the will of the gods… and Bowleg."

The Uncle brandished his sword and his relatives followed his example.

"You will **not** put the Curse on our innocent kinsman. If you try it, your blood will stain this green clearing deep red."

"But.. but.. the gods require it. I must perform the Curse ceremony, or the whole settlement will be damned for eternity." The Druid was whimpering, his face near to tears. "Maybe I could incant a kind of general Curse to the guilty, not directed at anyone in particular. I mean, if he's innocent, as you say, it wouldn't apply to him, would it?"

"If you must, but if you as much as whisper the name of my nephew, I'll cut your throat. And the rest of my family will chop you into little pieces." A roar of approval rose from the assembled Armours.

"OK. No names. Nothing specific. Everything very general and anonymous. Would that be OK?" Cathbad said.

The Uncle nodded, but kept his sword aloft. "Remember, I'm standing here with this ready in case you make any slip-ups."

The trembling Druid kneeled and raised his staff heavenward and began his incantation. "Oh gods, oh spirits of the land and the rivers, bear witness to this Curse. If any person thwarts the will of the gods, disrespects the priests or plots against the chieftains, may he be condemned to a life of anguish, a horrible and painful death, and everlasting torment." He paused, head bowed, for some moments before recommencing in a more normal voice. "That's it done then. Thomakin can toddle off now and we can get back to the encampment."

After many hugs and much shaking of hands, Thomakin set off in the direction indicated by his uncle and the Armours trekked back to the encampment with their crestfallen faces. They would all miss their young brother, but every one of them held in his heart the conviction that Thomakin was not lost to them for ever, and one day he would be back.

Once the forest clearing had been, so to speak, cleared, a small bent figure appeared from behind a tree. It was Beaufox, who could not have rested until he saw his adversary definitively banished. He had hidden there, unseen, to observe the proceedings. Which, in his view, were far from satisfactory. His intention had been that the upstart be flogged to within inches of his life and thrown into the wilderness, weak, naked and defenceless under a fatal curse from the gods. Instead the cur had been handed the best weapons and sent off with the good wishes of his kinsmen, and an irrelevant incantation from the Druid, the contents of which were more likely to condemn Beaufox himself than his sworn enemy. He feared matters were not at an end, and his battle with the pumped-up peasant may not yet be over.

When Joanie and I had finished the translation of this excerpt from Livy's histories, my friend's reaction was predictable. She was vehement in her condemnation of the two rogues, Beaufox and Cathbad, but particularly the latter. When I pointed out that calling the Druid a ruthless and heartless plotter would place her well within the remit of the Druid's Curse, she only laughed. Then she went on to label the priest a pure charlatan, whose gods were mere figments of the imagination, making matters worse. She was destined to pay for her indiscretions. It really pains me when people don't heed sound, sage advice.

7. GOOD BRITISH HOSPITALITY

At this point, the tale continues in two different directions, that taken by our hero Thomakin, and that followed by the cunning Beaufox Headman. But, for the moment, let us continue on the path of the righteous and find out what Livy has to tell us of the fate of the banished Thomakin Kobbler.

As he strolled away from his home territory and into the unknown, Thomakin must have thought that, after all, things could have been much worse. He was well-dressed, fully armed and the Druid's Curse had nothing to do with what he thought or what he had done. Then there was the little bag of coins that he had extorted from Beaufox for the boots; neither the Druid or the Headmans knew he still had that. To be honest, he felt more like a prosperous traveller then a destitute refugee. Oh yes, he had good grounds for hope, and if only fortune smiled a little kindly on him, things would be fine.

It was autumn, the trees and bushes were in fruit, and Thomakin regaled himself as he walked in the direction his uncle had told him was most likely to lead to safety and prosperity. He tapped the arrows in his belt; later he would shoot a small animal and have a sumptuous evening meal. And although he would miss his friends and family, he was starting a new life, and excitement was overcoming his regrets. His mind was racing. What sort of new people would he meet? How could he use his skills and knowledge to better himself in a new environment?

The problem with daydreaming is that it distracts you from what you should be really thinking about, and when Thomakin found himself in the centre of a circle of heavily armed gentlemen with painted faces, he inwardly cursed his inattention. His instinct was to reach for his sword, but he resisted it. The horde facing him undoubtedly looked fierce enough, but their swords were in their scabbards and their spears were at their sides, so he was in no immediate danger.

"Who are you and what right have you to invade our territory?" a gruff heavily bearded fellow called out.

"I be Thomakin Kobbler and I be just passing through."

"Passing through on the way to where?

Now, this was a tricky question, for, to be honest, Thomakin didn't have an answer to it. He had no idea where he was going. But the bearded fellow was eyeing him up suspiciously, and all around the circle hands were hovering over sword handles, so an answer was rather urgently required. "To the sea," he said. He had no idea where or even what the sea was, but he had overheard some visiting merchant talk about it and it was all that he could think of.

His answer did not seem to convince Beardie. "Hah! Am I supposed to believe that when you're armed to the teeth and carrying a bow and arrow? Are you a hunter or a soldier?"

"I be Thomakin Kobbler." Thomakin put a heavy stress on his surname. "Kobbler - a shoemaker."

"Then why all the weapons?"

"It be my hobby, like," Thomakin replied, "fightin' 'n huntin'"

"Hobby?"

"Aye, I does it like a sport."

"Sport?"

"Aye, in me free time, like. For fun."

Beardie shrugged his shoulders and looked bemused. It would seem, then, that those in this settlement had not yet learned basic Stone-Age economics: that the benefits of division of labour could lead to surpluses allowing individuals discretionary income and time to devote to the pursuit of pleasure. It would seem that, in the social system Beardie inhabited, there was no affluent family like the Kobblers. But he was saved from further embarrassment by the warrior next to him leaning over and whispering in his ear. Beardie listened, nodded and turned back to Thomakin.

"Thomakin Kobbler, you said your name was? That wouldn't be the Thomakin Kobbler. The one that knows his father was an Armour, who is well-liked in his settlement, and possesses formidable skill in wielding weapons?" Thomakin indicated thar he was indeed that very person. Beardie continued. "The Thomakin Kobbler who is so detested by that despotic rogue, Bowleg Headman, the ruler of his encampment. The same Thomakin Kobbler that the Armours and Hunters of your village have told us about?"

"I be he, sir. Indeed, I find myself in your parts as a result of an injustice done to me by Bowleg. I have been wrongly accused and banished from my settlement."

"Bowleg won't be your favourite person, then?"

"I hate him and be sworn to 'ave me revenge."

"Well, any enemy of Bowleg's is a friend of ours. Why don't you come along with us for a bit of supper and we'll have a little talk?"

Beardie led Thomakin through the forest and into a small village. They passed by a few small cultivated fields where the women were hard at work harvesting a meagre crop before they reached a settlement with makeshift wooden huts. A few old hags were keeping a watchful eye on a smattering of emaciated goats and cows, at the same time as sewing rough cloaks from sackcloth. Several children, not many, wandered around, carrying out menial tasks like collecting firewood or sweeping out the hovels. Thomakin was amazed; it was so different from his own settlement. They seemed so primitive. "Where be the other men?" he asked.

"Hunting and gathering," Beardie replied. "But come, take a seat and we'll have some food. My daughters, Abi and Obi, will attend to us. He shouted over to two rather attractive young women. "Food, daughters. Bring a feast for my guest."

The two men sat on the ground, for there was no table to be seen. The daughters put down their coarse needlework and looked over. When they saw the young Thomakin, they looked at each other and giggled, before running off into a nearby dwelling.

"All your people seem to do everything themselves. Why don't you do like we does and have each one concentrate on what he be best at? That way, they'd make more of everything and you'd all be better off," Thomakin suggested.

"An admirable economic argument, my friend, but it's just not our way. Besides, the villagers would get bored doing the same thing all the time."

Thomakin was about to tell him that the opposite was the case, and that everyone in the Bowleg encampment was proud of their particular skill, but the arrival of Abi and Obi interrupted him while he was drawing breath to speak. They were carrying bowls, roughly hewn out of old trees, filled with fruit, misshapen loaves of bread and rancid salty venison. They laid the feats on the ground between the two men. Then they too knelt down, one on either side of Thomakin.

"Tuck in," Beardie said, indicating the victuals with a wide spread of his arms.

Abi immediately picked a slightly soiled apple from a bowl and pushed against Thomakin's mouth, while at the same time entwining her spare arm around his neck. "Try this, you gorgeous young man."

He took a bite of the apple and pushed the rest of it out of the way, only to come face to face with a large venison sandwich. Obi, not to be outdone by her sister, had entangled his neck from the other direction and she too was presenting him with an offering. Finding himself imprisoned between the two young ladies, Thomakin opened his mouth to protest, and suddenly found bread and meat battling with the apple for space inside his mouth. "The daughters of Chief Beardie know how to satisfy a fit young chap like you," Obi said.

Unable to reply, Thomakin continued to munch and merely nodded.

"And once you have sated your hunger and thirst, you will find the delightful Abi ready to satisfy your other needs," Abi said, with a knowing wink.

"And indeed so will the delectable Obi," her sister added.

Thomakin swallowed his mouthful with a gulp that nearly choked him. "Ladies," he said, "it would not be right to choose one of you, for I could not do so without causing a rift between you."

"Well, have us both then. You're up for it, aren't you Obi?"

"You bet your sweet life I am, Abi."

To avert the new danger, Thomakin fell back on the old excuse that had served him so well in his own encampment. "It cannot be, ladies. I be pledged to monogamy. I have made a sacred oath to find one true love and be faithful to her for the whole of my life."

"What a bloody stupid custom. How can you ever have any fun?" Abi said.

"Are all the men in your village like you then?" Obi asked.

"No, I be an exception. But times are changing. Times be coming when women will no longer put up with being used for pleasure and then discarded."

"We don't mind, do we, Abi?"

"No way. You can take and leave me any time you like, handsome stranger."

Thomakin smiled graciously at the two young women. "I'm sorry, girls. I have given vows to the gods, and I must sadly decline your kind offers."

"Oh well, come on, Abi. Let's leave Dad and our high and mighty visitor to their supper. There's no fun to be had here."

"Too right, Obi." But as they were leaving, Abi looked back at Thomakin. "But if you change your mind, you know where I am."

When they had gone, Thomakin turned to his host. "Don't you think you should encourage your girls to be a little less free with their favours?"

"Not at all, son. It encourages diversity in the gene pool. But let us move on to more important matters. I think you and I could work together to overcome the despot Bowleg. I'd like you to help me by training my men as soldiers to take him on."

Thomakin thought for a few moments. "No, I'm sorry, sir. The Armours be responsible for the defence of my community, no matter who be in control. You're asking me to bring destruction on my own family. I just can't do it. I'll get me revenge on Bowleg Headman, but not this way. I will continue with my quest to find another solution. I hope you understand."

"Of course I do, son. But we share the same goals. When you have a plan to eliminate the hateful Bowleg, my people and I will help you all we can. But come, eat up your supper. And then I suggest you accept the hospitality of my house to rest for the night before continuing in your search."

The thought of sharing space overnight with Beardie's two daughters was just too much for Thomakin, so as soon as he gracefully could, he excused himself, thanked his host and set off back into the forest before night came.

8. THE NEW JOB

Darkness came soon after Thomakin left Beardie's encampment, but Thomakin ploughed on. He had no intention of camping down anywhere close, where he might be at the mercy of any nocturnal impulses that may overtake Abi and Obi. When he judged he was safely out of their range, he lay down under a tree and fell asleep.

Even the dodgy Roman historian Livy admits that his account of the dream Thomakin had that night may be more legend than fact. Who can verify the imaginations of another, whether they be had while awake or asleep? Yet, in spite of its doubtful provenance, I feel compelled to include it here because of its bearing on subsequent events. It is for you, sir (or madam), to make up your own minds.

In his dream, the forest Thomakin found himself in was dark and eery. Not that much different from the one he was in in reality, you might be thinking. Not so. In his dream, the chill of the night was several degrees icier than he had ever experienced before. The whistling sounds of the wind became the voices of predatory ghosts creeping up on him. The gnarled trunks of trees were transformed into hungry monsters and dragons. Although Thomakin was desperate to flee to safety, he was transfixed by invisible bonds and forced to wait in terror for whatever fate had in store for him. As he cowered behind a bush, a group of shadowy figures approached, emitting a monotonous chant with menacing overtones.

They drew closer and he recognised them as a procession of Druid priests, one of whom was known to him. It was the same Cathbad who had banished him from his homeland. He seemed to have fallen out of favour with his colleagues, for he was being dragged reluctantly by the chains that bound his arms to his body. When the group arrived in front of the hidden Thomakin, they pushed Cathbad to his knees and formed a circle around him, waving their staffs and spitting angrily in his direction. The hissing that filled the forest air was so vehement that Thomakin almost felt sorry for poor Cathbad, for the young exile's capacity for forgiveness was unbounding.

The tallest among them raised an arm and silence replaced the vile sounds of hatred. A voice boomed out, echoing around the trees. "Cathbad, you have failed us. You have put the safety of our religion in jeopardy and incurred the wrath of the gods. You will have to atone for your sins and right the wrongs you have committed. Do you swear to carry out your new instructions to the letter?"

Through his sobs, the whimpering Druid acquiesced. "Yes, Great One. Whatever you say, Great One."

"You failed in your task to rid us of the rebellious and dangerous Thomakin Kobbler. He is still alive and at large when he should be dead and buried. The gods have designated Beaufox Headman to correct your error. You will offer him any assistance he requires. You must be his constant support and obey his every command. Do you promise?"

"Yes, Great One. I promise, Great One. Whatever you say, Great One."

There followed some unmentionable ritual abominations to Cathbad's body, involving priestly daggers, heavy staffs and the odd burning torch. Then he was led away, wailing and moaning, and repeating his mantra: "Yes, Great One. I promise, Great One. Whatever you say, Great One". His undying loyalty was thus assured.

When Thomakin woke up, the sun's rays were projecting stripes on the forest floor and the day was dawning comfortably warm. In the heat and light, the terror of his dream dissipated, but he found himself considering in what way he was 'rebellious and dangerous'. He wondered if those Druids in his dream knew something he didn't. Ah well, he was not one to let his nocturnal imaginations trouble him for long. Shrugging it all off, he set out towards his future. He kept the sun on his left, for he recalled the Hunters telling him that if he set off in that direction in the morning he would eventually find the sea. As he walked, he gathered and ate the fruits of the forest for breakfast.

His mind was filled with a variety of vague notions about his future. Robbed of his two families by the treacherous Headmans, how would he survive? It was unlikely to be by shoemaking, for he knew other Kobbler families would never take on a worker from outside. But the offer from

Beardie had opened up a possibility. His prowess with weapons might be his key to prosperity, although he could never consider using them against his own kin. But in a distant land, far from where his kinsmen would ever wander, might he not embark on a military career? He resolved to keep his mind open for such an opportunity.

As if on cue, his call to arms arrived sooner than he had expected. A loud screeching suddenly penetrated the forest, and Thomakin could discern certain words being uttered in a distraught and anxious fashion. *Rogues, vagabonds, thieves* and *scoundrels* rang out through the trees with monotonous regularity. Thomakin could only conclude that some poor wayfarer was in the throes of being robbed. For a young man to whom any evil was intolerable, such an outrage could not be allowed to continue. Drawing his sword from its sheath, he rushed forth in the direction of the commotion.

He soon came upon the terrible scene. While one painted savage with a large knife was threatening a wizened old man, another was rummaging among the containers strapped to a beast of burden tethered nearby. Our hero's resounding war cry dispatched the latter, empty handed, into the forest, allowing Thomakin to turn his attention to the bolder and more foolhardy villain. The brave rescuer's sword swished through the air and the offending knife fell to the ground, with a severed hand still attached to it. The amputee gazed momentarily at the bleeding stump, before emitting a terrified wail and rushing headlong into the undergrowth, abandoning his lost appendage on the forest floor.

The old wayfarer was effuse in his gratitude. "Oh, brave stranger, you have saved my life. How can I repay you?. How vulnerable a merchant is, travelling the byways of England alone in these troubled times? Verily, I am an old fool, undertaking such a journey unprotected in my advancing years. I should be past such foolishness. But one has to make one's living, has one not? However, I am resolved not continue with this stupidity. The next time, I shall employ a bodyguard to accompany me. Indeed, but for your intervention there would not be a next time. To what do I owe my good fortune, young sir? What brings you to the depths of the forest in time to be my saviour?"

"I be the victim of profound treachery, old man. Banished from my settlement and condemned to find a new life in a world I know nothing of."

"Then I warrant you'll be in need of gainful employment, young fellow."

"Indeed, I so be."

"Well, fortune is smiling upon both of us today. For here are you in need of work, and I in need of a bodyguard. And have you not just demonstrated how well qualified you are for such a position? Come, young sir, and throw in your lot with mine, and together we will conquer the world."

Thomakin was soundly tempted by the offer, and only slightly suspicious. "I be happy to be your bodyguard, but there be the question of the terms and conditions of my employment."

"Then let me suggest that we continue on our way together, and as we walk let us discuss your remuneration and other benefits. I am sure we can find a mutually rewarding accommodation. Just let me collect my beast and my belongings and we'll be off. By the way, my name is Tiberius."

And so the party set off in the direction of the sea, with the laden beast at the end of a rope being led by his master. In front of the pack horse was Thomakin, the newly-appointed bodyguard, with the fatherly arm of the merchant Tiberius draped over his shoulder.

9 THE VILLA

In the days it took for Thomakin and Tiberius to reach the old merchant's home, the pair of them formed a close friendship. As they journeyed, they talked together at length, discoursing on a wide variety of subjects. Not the least of these was Tiberius's family and business situation. It soon became apparent that the old merchant had taken a real shine to young Thomakin, and was quickly forming plans to make him more than just a bodyguard.

"I worry about my young daughter, you know. Who will look after her when I'm gone?" he confided to Thomakin.

"You know who your children be?" the younger man asked, somewhat surprised.

"Ah, I know that you're thinking. But you see, we Romans do not behave like people in many of your villages do; we don't run around sleeping with anyone who'll have us. Well, not officially, anyway. We pick out one woman and live together to build our family. But I suppose your people won't know anything about that?"

"Well, I does," Thomakin replied, and went on to recount the story of his own parents. This piece of information seemed to endear him even more to the merchant.

"Ah well, in that case, young sir, you are the ideal person to take care of my little girl, should the need arise. For you understand well the concept of family ties. It is hard for we merchants, trading alone in strange lands where our protective armies have never been, all for the good of the Republic. For we could be cut down at any time by evil enemies, but with you there to look after my little Lustia and my business, my mind will be at rest."

The prospect of being handed the responsibility of a little child filled Thomakin with dismay, for he himself had just reached adulthood. "Surely, sir, she has a mother and brothers who will take care of her."

"Alas no. For Lustia is my one and only. You see, young man, I made the mistake of putting career before family, and my dearest Aurelia and I did not become a couple until later in life. Always a difficult situation in these barbarian lands, where competent medical facilities are hard to find. To my despair, my darling Aurelia died giving birth to our firstborn."

"So you be having no other offspring, then?"

"None that I know about. I may have a few dozen scattered around these lands, for you know how things are done here. But they will have been absorbed into your system of extended families."

Thomakin found himself trapped. As we discovered earlier, he was a young man of exceptional kindness of heart and a sucker for a sad tale, and the thought of an abandoned orphan was more than he could bear. "I would not leave your child alone and unprotected in the world, Tiberius, but as for your business, I know nothing of merchanting."

The old fellow put his arm around Thomakin's shoulders and squeezed. "You need have no fears about that, Thomakin. I will teach you everything, and, though I hope to live for many years yet, you will inherit the business from me. From now on, please call me 'father' Tiberius."

And so it came about that our hero went from being a poor banished shoemaker with no prospects to being a member of a notable family and heir to a successful enterprise.

As the days passed, Thomakin learned that Tiberius the merchant was on his way home, taking the goods he had accumulated back to where it would be stored for 'export'. Thomakin had no idea what 'export' meant, but being a young fellow of infinite patience and wary of accentuating his ignorance, he said nothing, confident all would be revealed in the fullness of time.

"Aye boy, the boats will be here soon and we will be sending all this stuff off by sea."

"That be very interesting, father Tiberius, for I have never seen the sea."

The older man smiled. "Well, it will be a surprise for you."

In fact, not one, but three surprises were lying in wait for Thomakin, and each of them would change his life forever.

The next day, the pair of them pulled the reluctant pack horse up a sharp incline and at its summit Thomakin's first surprise was revealed to him. Below them were the long sandy beaches of the coast, and beyond a wide expanse of sea. Thomakin gasped at the splendour of the scene. He was familiar with water from the river that ran though his settlement, but he had never imagined there could be so much of it.

"So much water," he said, out loud, "I be glad not to be going there."

"Oh, but yes you are, my friend. For when I take the merchandise across the water, you will be coming with me. How else will you learn the intricacies of my profession?"

This was Thomakin's first surprise, and he couldn't decide whether to welcome it or not. It was an adventure, but was it an adventure too far? The sight of all that water gave him the heebie-jeebies.

"Come," said Tiberius, "my home is close by."

They walked on a little bit further and a large settlement came into view. "There she is, home sweet home," Tiberius announced. It was a settlement the like of which Thomakin had never before seen, although, to be fair, up to then he hadn't got about much. There were four large square wooden edifices in a row, each with straw roofs. The usual holes for the smoke were missing from them. Nearby was large square building built in a kind of stone Thomakin was not familiar with. He could not begin to imagine its purpose. The whole encampment was surrounded by a fence of wooden stakes, creating a protective ring around all the buildings. It was so different from the random collection of roundhouses where he had lived until misfortune overtook him.

"Which of these huts is yours?" he asked.

"All of them. They are the warehouses where we store the merchandise while they are awaiting transport. The other building is the house, or, as we call it, the villa. You'll find it very comfortable. Come along."

Having been amazed twice, Thomakin wondered what else was in store for him. Nothing, he hoped, but he was wrong.

They made their way down to the settlement, and Tiberius knocked on the wooden gate with his staff. A few seconds later it was opened, and they passed through. An old man, with skin darker than any Thomakin had ever seen, closed and bolted the gate behind them.

"You're back, Master," the old fellow said, bowing at the merchant.

"Indeed I am, Gaius. Take care of the horse and the contents of the paniers. We're going to the villa. Come, Thomakin."

Thomakin followed the old merchant, who seemed to have acquired a new air of youthful authority as he strode towards the house. It was, he supposed, the confidence of man who was master of his environment. As they approached the building, Tiberius called out, "Lustia, Lustia, Daddy's home."

A vision emerged from the villa. A comely wench of around his own age with bright flowing hair, dressed in a long garment made of a material finer than any Thomakin had ever come across. "Ave, Daddy, you've come home," the vision uttered. So this was little, defenceless Lustia. He had been expecting a child of seven or eight years of age; this wasn't what he had signed up for.

The young lady bent forward and kissed her father on the cheek, smiling. But then she turned to face Thomakin and the smile was replaced by a formidable glare that radiated hostility. She didn't look like anyone that would need protection; she could probably protect herself very well, and him too if the need ever arose. He was regretting his promise to her father already.

But there was one good thing about Lustia. She smelt absolutely delightful.

10 CLEAN UP

"Daddy, you stink," Lustia said.

"I'm sorry, sweetheart. I've been traveling for weeks in this primitive country. The standards of hygiene are intolerable."

"Go and have a bath. And take your friend with you; he smells even worse than you do."

"Of course, my little one. And could you have the slaves prepare some nourishment? My friend Thomakin and I have been living off the land and we're in need of a good feed. Oh and send a couple of the slave boys along to the Bath room for our massages. Come, Thomakin."

The pair walked past Lustia into the villa. Thomakin was amazed, he had never imagined such luxury could be possible. The room he had just entered had a hole in the roof, but where he would have expected a fire there was a little rectangular pond full of water. The pond was surrounded by objects the like of which he had never before encountered. He would later learn some of them were called tables and chairs, and others that bore some resemblance to people were designated as statues. "This is this atrium, and the living quarters are beyond." But first, we will go the baths to carry out our ablutions," Tiberius informed him.

Thomakin was confused by so many new words. In modern times we are used to the significant expansion in vocabulary needed to match the meteoric speed to technological development, but in that era the rate of scientific advance was slow and laboured, specially in those backward regions now known as Britain. But the word 'bath' intrigued Thomakin, for both Tiberius and Lustia had used it, and he sought erudition. "Tell me, father Tiberius, what is a bath?"

"Ah, it is an important Roman ceremony, which in the Eternal City is normally conducted in public buildings, but as we are the sole Romans in your land, I have had constructed a smaller domestic version at great expense. But come and see for yourself, for you will find the experience most invigorating."

Tiberius led Thomakin into a large room with three pools full of water, with a pair of low stone benches at one end. Beside them were some large stone urns. The host explained, "the nearest pool is the Tepidarium, then we have the Caldarium and, at the end there, the Frigidarium. Throw off those dirty smelly clothes, there are tunics and togas waiting for us once we have had the massage." So saying, the old merchant stepped out of his clothes and immersed himself in the first pool. "Come on, Thomakin," he shouted, "the water's lovely."

Thomakin had never before encountered such odd behaviour, but if the old fellow was doing it he supposed it would not be fatal, so he disrobed and joined him in the pool. It was a pleasant sensation, for the warmth of the water was soothing and comfortable. Thomakin stretched out his limbs and luxuriated, but all too soon his host announced. "Enough of this, Caldarium next," and stepped out of the first pool and into the second. Thomakin immediately followed.

The water was a lot warmer: so hot, in fact, it was almost unbearable. But Thomakin soon became accustomed to the heat and to be honest he found it even more pleasant than the first pool. As he lay back, wallowing in luxury, two young teenage boys entered, each carrying a pile of vestments and sat on the benches waiting.

"Frigidarium now, both at the same time. Thomakin," Tiberius said. He got out of the pool, then took his guest's hand and pulled him out too. They stood by the side of the pool, hand in hand, until Tiberius said, "One, two, three…jump."

Thomakin thought he was going to die. His breath was taken from him, and he felt his muscles tighten up and lock. Tiberius was smiling. "Invigorating, is it not? But enough is enough." He pulled his guest out of this pool too, and poor Thomakin stood shivering beside the benches. But the effect soon passed, and he felt his body return to normal, and the tingle he was feeling seemed strangely satisfying. "Lie yourself down on the bench, face down, and the boys will bring your body back to life," Tiberius ordered.

Thomakin did as he was told, and looked up to see one of the boys dip his hand into one of the urns and withdraw them, dripping of some viscous oily substance. Thomakin recognised the smell; the same scent that his projected protegee had been radiating when he had met her at the door of the villa. Then he felt the hands on his back and the rubbing, the pulling, the squeezing and the pounding began. Was he being tortured? Eventually the ordeal ended, and he heard a voice saying, "Sit up, master. Here are your clothes."   He sat up to face the young lad offering him an armful of white vestments.

"Pull the tunic over your head first, then I'll show you how the toga is worn. Of course, back home we only wear one or the other, but it's so cold here we have to wear both."

Once he was dressed, Thomakin felt wonderful. Never had he been so fresh, so sweet-smelling and so relaxed. This weird ritual was one he could easily get used to. As he followed Tiberius back to the atrium he resolved to introduce the ritual into his own house, should he ever be allowed to return there.

When they entered the atrium, Lustia was waiting for them, lying on a long low bench. In front of her, a long low table was creaking under the weight of a variety of different foods, laid out in bowls. Pitchers of wine and drinking vessels were scattered around, among the food. Tiberius indicated one of the two other benches beside the table to his guest, saying, "Just lie down on that one, boy, and tuck in. Not a bad spread, Lustia, it'll do to start with. I presume the slaves have more ready in the Culina, for we won't be long with this lot, will we, Thomakin?"

The young lady looked over at the now more respectable guest and frowned "Daddy, who is this Thomakin exactly?"

"Oh, sorry my little one. Didn't I introduce him? Lustia, this is Thomakin, whom I have just appointed as my assistant and who will be your guardian should anything happen to me."

"I be pleased to meet you," Thomakin said.

His bath and the Roman attire had not diminished the young woman's disdain. "I'm sure you are," she said. Then she turned to her father. "Daddy, I hope you're not trying to marry me off."

"Excuse me," Thomakin interrupted, "But what be 'marry' please?"

The Lustian eyebrows were raised to the heavens.

Her father stepped in with an explanation. "In our culture, when a gentleman chooses a lady as the love of his life, the bond is celebrated by a ceremony known as a wedding. The couple are then married, the gentleman becomes the husband, and the lady his wife."

Thomakin thought that an excellent custom and resolved to take advantage of it when he himself found 'the one'. But he also saw a way out of his unwisely accepted commitment. "In that case, in spite of my promise to you, Tiberius, when the young lady finds a husband, I shall, of course, defer to him."

Surprisingly, this did not appear to please the young Roman lady. "Hold on! Hold on! You haven't even begun to fulfil your obligations to me, and you're trying to wriggle out of them already."

"But I assumed that would be your wish, miss."

"Don't try to tell me what my wishes are, barbarian."

Now if Beaufox, or even Bowleg, had spoken to Thomakin in such a fashion, he would not have put up with it. No sir, he would not. But at heart, as we have already said, Thomakin's soul was filled with love and kindness for all (except the Headmans). He pushed his annoyance to the back of his mind. "Indeed I would not dare, miss. I will be by your side, as your protector, as long as you desire my attentions, for I did so promise your father. I be your humble servant, miss."

His offer must have taken the wind out of her sails, for she did not rush forth with further insults. Instead, she deigned to offer him a smile. It was one of those sly smiles, patronising more than amiable, a veneer of politeness rather than a hand of friendship. But it was perhaps the first signs of the melting of the ice-maiden. Eventually she found suitable words. "Of course you are. But we'll have to do something about your grammar. Latin is, of course, the gold standard in communication, and English an undisciplined and barbaric language, but even it has its rules. If you are to have discourse with me, you will have to learn the correct conjugation of the verb 'to be'.

11 SUCCESSION PLANNING

In Rome, as Joanie and I worked together in the library of the Antiquity Centre on the translation of Livy's account of the first meeting between Thomakin and Lustia, Joanie was becoming more and more agitated. Eventually, her heart could not hold in any more indignation and it burst forth in a mighty explosion. "The cow!" she screamed. "How could she treat the wonderful Thomakin in such a fashion? If I could get my hands on her, I would wring her tiny neck." I could see eyes being raised among the other researchers in the library, and indeed some were making moves that indicated they were preparing to confront us.

In order to avoid any unpleasantness, I took Joanie by the hand and whispered in her ear. "Let's take a break, dearest. It's lunchtime anyway. We can go to a nearby ristorante and sample one of the delicious pasta delights offered by this city. And I can update you on the latest progress on my translation of the etchings on the Stonehenge Stone Hoard." I whisked her out of there before she could raise any protest. I had the feeling that she was showing a somewhat unprofessional interest in our iron-age hero, and I thought that diverting her attention to the events happening back in the Headmans' settlement would clam her down. How wrong can you be?

A word of warning, sir (or madam). Historical research is not an exact science, and the chronology of events are often difficult to discern. There is no way to tie up exactly the evidence from the Stones to the historical account by the Roman Livy, but I would suggest that the events I am about to describe occurred some little time after those I have just recounted. I apologise for placing them a little out of sequence, and I can only say in mitigation that, at that point in our work together, I had a burning need to soothe my good friend Joanie's angry soul.

In the days following Thomakin's banishment from the village, Beaufox devoted himself to considered reflection. It was evident from the handling of the Kobbler trial that the Headman dynasty and its power over the community was under threat. His father, Bowleg, was not up to the task of leading the villagers. And if Bowleg was a problem, his big brother Bo-Ring would be a disaster. Something needed to be done, and there was no one but he, Beaufox, who could do it.

But now was not the time. Beaufox realised that he had not yet reached maturity, and if his incompetent father and useless elder brother were to be removed, the population would not accept him as successor. Some sort of Regency would be imposed, under one of his devious uncles or cousins, none of whom Beaufox would have trusted with the care of a village chicken. Patience was the order of the day, and for the moment he was to devote his time to scheming, planning and preparing.

Beaufox realised that he would need the help of some of the peasantry. This he would secure, not by friendship, but by fear, because he had to start as he meant to go on. It was a habit of the male members of the Headman family to participate in hunting expeditions, not in order to feed the inhabitants of the settlement, but as a diversion from the daily grind of ordering people about. Any one of these expeditions would provide ample opportunity for dastardly deeds, but an accomplice would be needed. So Beaufox resolved to seek out a weak-minded but adequately proficient member of the Hunter clan and intimidate him.

Of course, his ascension to power would require the acquiescence of the gods, so he would have to get the Druid on his side. Cathbad had gone on a pilgrimage just after the Kobbler trial, claiming that he needed to renew his faith and his pastoral commitment, and that in any case the priestly hierarchy had summoned him to a meeting. As soon as he returned, the Beaufox sought him out, and engaged him in conversion with the intention of finding an indiscretion or fault that the young Prince could use to manipulate the cleric. He needn't have bothered; he found the Druid unusually deferential and obliging.

"Ah, your young eminence, how wonderful of you to grace me with your presence. Can I be of service?" the Druid said as Beaufox approached him.

"Not right now, priest, but you may be called upon to do something for me in the near future."

"It will be my pleasure, your greatness. Whatever you wish. Anything at all."

"Anything? At all?" Beaufox was puzzled by this sudden willingness to be of service. Had the Druid been so accommodating earlier, his enemy Thomakin Kobbler would no longer be in existence.

"Indeed, your magnificence. For I am resolved to fulfil your every wish. Yours above all others."

"Above all others? All?"

"There is no one who could take precedence over you, my exalted one. You are Number One."

"Well, that's good to know, Cathbad. And be assured, your services will be called upon. But if you fail in your tasks, my wrath will descend upon you. On the other hand, if you succeed, you will be well rewarded."

"No reward is sought, great one. The opportunity to serve is all I seek." At this, the Druid bowed so low that his beard scraped the soil. Beaufox resisted the temptation to place his boot on his upended backside and push him over. Instead he walked away, thinking to himself, what a turn up for the books, something must have got into him.

Time passed. Beaufox's feet grew to fill the ornamental boots he had stolen from his elder brother, and he wore them to his own coming-of-age ceremony. Adulthood was upon him; there could be no question now of an unwanted Regency; it was time to act.

The day after Beaufox's coming of age, he had arranged a hunting party for all the Headmans. The Hunters would accompany them into the woods and they would kill a wild boar which the women of the village would cook. Then the whole settlement would participate in a great celebration of Beaufox's arrival into majority. Bowleg thought the idea was overly generous to the peasants, but his son insisted, saying that it was his celebration and he would have it in the manner he thought best.

As the hunting party headed into the forest, Beaufox took Nobrane Hunter to one side and explained what the serf was required to do. There would be no question of disobedience; the young huntsman was bound to his master by a mixture of fear and admiration that Beaufox had carefully built up over the years. Once he was fully satisfied that his dull conspirator had understood the instruction, he called over his father and elder brother. "Dad, Bo-Ring, here's the plan. You two are to have the honour of killing today's prey. You will wait here in this clearing, weapons at the ready, while the rest of us go into the forest, locate a suitable beast, and drive it towards you. It will be a mere trifle for you to bring down the disorientated animal and receive the acclamation of the whole population, as indeed is your due."

Bo-Ring looked rather doubtful, for he was not known as a great hunter. But old Bowleg was bursting with pride and anticipation. It would be no problem for him. He had never actually bagged a boar before, But had he not hunted extensively many times, and with some success? But unlike his wily son Beaufox, Bowleg did not realise that a wild angry male pig was an entirely different adversary from a baby deer or a rabbit.

Leaving the leader and his heir to prepare themselves, the rest of the party disappeared into the forest. Immediately,

Beaufox sent the others off to search for game, while he and Nobrane made their way to a secret cave. Inside this hiding place a large angry boar was tethered by two ropes. "Still here, good." Beaufox said. "We've kept it here for two days since we caught it. You have not fed it, I hope." Nobrane nodded. "Perfect, Nobrane. It will be ravenous and furious. I think it will do the trick."

Beaufox loosened one of the ropes, and pulled it tight. "You do the same, Nobrane. Keep the rope tight like I am doing. I will stop the beast coming towards you, and you will it stop it coming towards me." In this manner, they dragged the boar close to the edge of the forest close to the clearing where Beaufox's relatives were waiting, our of sight. Beaufox tied his rope to a tree, and Nobrane did likewise, immobilising the animal.

They then picked up some nearby branches and began beating the poor beast into a frenzy, before cutting the ropes and sending it off in the direction of the clearing. When the boar saw the two hunters it behaved exactly as Beaufox had expected it would. It ran straight at Bowleg, who was struggling to pull his sword from its sheath, and trampled him to death. Bo-Ring turned and fled, but he had only gone a few yards when the irate pig caught up and he received the same treatment as his father. By the time Beaufox and his accomplice reached the clearing, the victorious animal was feasting on the remains of its quarry.

Beaufox and Nobrane hurled their spears at the beast, and it fell dead in mid-feast. Victuals were needed for his celebration, after all.

"Tie its legs together, Nobrane, so we can carry it away. I'll go and fetch the others."

Nobrane nodded in the direction of Beaufox's two departed family members. "What about them two, boss?"

"We're not going to eat them. The big pig's been at them, for goodness sake."

"No, no, no. I was thinking about the usual formalities."

"Oh, I'll send the Druid round with some of the Scavenger family tomorrow to clear up the mess and carry out the necessary rituals. In the meantime, time for the party."

12 THE CORONATION

As I read out my translation of these events to Joanie over our spaghetti, I could see she was beginning to get a bit agitated. If I had had any sense, I would have stopped then and there. But you know how it is; you get carried away with a story and just can't stop. Oh well!

The hunting party carried the boar back to the settlement, leaving their former ruler and his heir for the vultures. After Beaufox had finished instructing the ladies of the village on the preparations required for his party, the idea came to him that he had a duty to inform his mother about what had occurred in the forest. So, rather reluctantly, he shuffled over to the family roundhouse.

"Hey Mum, I'm back."

"Very nice, dear," his mother replied, without looking up from the garment she was sewing.

"Bit of bad news, I'm afraid." His mother continued with her sewing.

"It's the old man, Mumsy. He won't be coming back."

"Very good, dear." Like all the other Headmans, his mum had been afflicted with the genetic defects of the family, and in her case it had affected her brain.

"You don't understand, Mummy. He won't be coming back, ever. There was an accident on the hunt."

His mother uttered an expletive in the language of the ancient Britons. "Damn needles, they always break when you need them most."

"Mum, pay attention. Your husband is dead. You're a widow."

"Well, I dare say I'll get by all right. Be a darling and go and see if you can find me a spare needle."

"There's more, Mum. It's about your first born."

"You mean boring Bo-Ring. The weak-minded wimp. What's he done now?"

"Well, I don't think he was quite up to the task of boar hunting. Just like Dad. They didn't seem to realise they were supposed to kill the boar, not the other way round."

"Hmmm!" his mother said, and then raised her voice. "Hey, Verica, be a good daughter and bring me a sharp bone needle from your workbox."

The said Verica came running into the room and handed her mother the requested needle. Then she noticed her brother. "Oh back already," she said. "Hunting any good."

"Not bad, Verica. Got a nice boar. Lost your Dad and brother, though."

"They never know where they are, those two."

"No, I mean we've lost them for good. They didn't get the boar; the boar got them."

"Oh, I see." Verica thought for a moment. "I suppose this means you'll be the new chieftain now."

"I never thought, sister. I suppose you're right," Beaufox lied.

Oh well, if the Druid's going to anoint you tonight, it'll be a better party than we were expecting. Mum and I will just get on with our sewing. Make sure we've got something really nice to wear for the occasion. You run along and make your preparations."

"Yes, dear. Run off and do all those manly sort of things your Daddy used to do. It'll all be up to you now, son," his mother said, before getting back to her sewing.

The party that evening was a big success. A multiple celebration, in fact. There was a sumptuous feast of pig meat and the mead was flowing freely. The villagers were rid of the hated Bowleg and his spindly son. Not that they liked Beaufox that much, but at that point they thought he was the least of all possible evils. And a Druid ritual always went down well. There wasn't a new chieftain anointment every day, so when Cathbad the Druid stood up and waved his staff, the whole community listened in rapt attention. He was wearing his most ornate vestments, so they knew it was a special event.

"Worshippers, the gods have spoken. Our erstwhile leader, Bowleg, had been taken from us, together with his appointed successor, Bo-Ring. But let us not be sad; this is not a misfortune, but a blessing. For Bowleg was an incompetent and his son, Bo-Ring, a degenerate. But fortune has smiled on our community. Circumstances have thrust Beaufox, beloved of the gods and the choice of the brotherhood of Druids, to prominence. Great things lie in wait for King Beaufox and his followers. Our forgotten little settlement is soon to be the most celebrated throughout the land, and our leader the lord of the world. Be like me, follow the gods. And follow the great Beaufox."

Beaufox was well pleased. The priest had delivered the speech just as he had instructed. And it seemed to have gone down well. His subjects could now look to being people of importance, people of influence (as long as they did what he told them). There was a unanimous swelling of wellbeing permeating everywhere.

Well, not quite everywhere. Not in the little Roman ristorante in the present day. As I told the story, Joanie's face was hardening and she almost choked on her spaghetti... twice. I sensed an explosion was coming and I wasn't wrong. For the sake of decorum, I won't repeat her outburst word for word, but the names she reserved for Beaufox, the Druid and their gods were considerably less than complementary. When I reminded her it was unwise to invoke the wraths of deities, even if you don't believe in them, she turned on me. I whisked her out of that ristorante and back to the library before she resorted to violence.

13 GAUL

On the way back to the library, I availed myself of the opportunity to have a serious word with Joanie. "Listen, Joanie," I said, " you have to get a grip of yourself. You have to stop all this emotional involvement in the lives of those historical figures we are researching. We're serious historians, for goodness sake. Truth and impartiality have to be our watchwords. Otherwise no one will take our work seriously." I think my words had the desired effect. Joanie behaved impeccably in the library of the Roman Republic Antiquity Centre. For the next few days anyway.

According to Livy, Thomakin was not given long to enjoy Roman Villa life and the dubious pleasure of sharing it with the luscious Lustia. Within a few days, two craft beached up on the coast near the villa, and the task of loading Tiberius's merchandise commenced. The captains of the vessels oversaw the process, promising the merchant that they would be utterly fastidious in ensuring that his property was stored in a safe and shipshape fashion. Tiberius seemed to trust them completely, for he devoted the two days it took to load up the boats to planning the trip.

Lustia had her contribution to the planning too. "Thomakin will share the guest cabin on the boat with us, of course," she suggested to her father. Her father raised his eyebrows. "He has to stay close to protect me," she added.

"Lustia, *I* am there to protect you. Thomakin is just a back-up in case anything happens to me."

"Oh, I see." She seemed deflated, but not for long. "But Daddy, he needs to practice. You wouldn't leave me in the care of someone totally inexperienced, would you."

"Daughter, Thomakin is very experienced and has no need of practice. He is accomplished in the use of weapons, and, indeed, he has even saved my life. No, he will berth down with the crew as is the custom." Lustia's look suggested that the kind of experience she had in mind was very different from that her Dad was talking about. But her father's words had an air of finality about them, so she did not pursue the matter.

In fact she had another plan; and she appraised Thomakin of it that very afternoon. "Barbarian," she said, "it has struck me that you will be severely disadvantaged in being my father's assistant due to your lack of knowledge of the Latin language. I have decided to rectify that, and I will start to teach you right away."

Now, as we know, Thomakin had only recently begun his travels and hadn't really gone all that far, and the concept of foreign languages was somewhat alien to him. He had no idea what Lustia was talking about, but being the kind and accommodating person he was, he readily agreed to her suggestion.

"We shall begin," Lustia announced, "with the conjugation of the present tense of the verb 'amare.' It means 'to love'."

Thomakin wondered what relevance such a word could possibly have to his role as a merchant's helper and bodyguard. He also wondered why she insisted on him looking her straight in the eye and repeating time after time the first person singular version.

"Amo, amo, amo…" He went on and on, and he could see by the brilliance in her moist eyes that she was pleased with him. He was glad to be making her happy.

Joanie didn't react well to this part of the tale, but at least her reaction this time was somewhat subdued. "The hussy," she whispered.

Thomakin, Tiberius and Lustia's voyage across what we now know as the English Channel was uneventful, and they arrived at little settlement on the coast of Gaul after two days. Lustia had kept the young Briton hard at his language lessons, although he did not feel he had progressed much beyond *amo, amo, amo.*

Their port of call was a small enclave of Roman traders, who were delighted to see their friend Tiberius back unharmed from treacherous lands. *(It is not clear from Livy's text where this settlement was, but it would be appear to be somewhere near what we now call Brittany or the Loire regions)*

A sumptuous reception awaited them there. Tiberius's less adventurous colleagues had decided not to venture overseas, but to remain in Gaul comfortably close to the protection of Julius Caesar's army. Even although the Gallic wars were in full swing, they had felt that this was a more prudent option than to risk life and limb on a treacherous sea-crossing and then a barbarian territory. But they were overjoyed at the safe return of their fellow merchant, and full of admiration for his courage.

"I say, old chap, you're back in one piece. How was it over there in the dark lands?" he was asked.

"Ah, you know…" Tiberius answered, shrugging emphatically. He was a crafty old character, and he didn't want to impart how well he had done for himself thanks to the absence of any competition.

"Maybe you made the right decision. Been hard here, old boy, what with that Vercingetorix up to his tricks, and giving Julius a hell of a time trying to keep him under control," one of the traders announced.

"And now that Julius has sloped off back to Rome for yet another tribute, we've been left to deal with the rogue Gallic leader by ourselves. It's costing us a fortune in gifts to keep the bearded barbarian sweet, I can tell you," another of the welcoming committee added.

"But enough of business, boys" said an older man who seemed to be the leader of the group. "My, how your little Lustia has blossomed. Time she was fixed up with a husband, what! And what a chance it would be to unite our two commercial empires, Tiberius. My little Brutus would just be the right age for her."

This remark was not well received by the intended bride. "Brutus the Brute? No way am I letting him anywhere near me."

The hopeful father of the bridegroom smiled knowingly and pointed to Thomakin, who had been hanging around in the background, feeling left out of things due to his still poor grasp of Latin. "And who is this? Have you brought back a British slave?"

"Oh, no, not at all," Tiberius replied. "I mean, I know there's good money in human trafficking, but my view is that the resentment it causes among the indigenous population outweighs any quick profits you might make. No, Thomakin is no slave; he's a free man and I've employed him as my assistant."

This produced a wave of indignation and amazement among the gathering. "Your assistant? But he's a barbarian. How could he ever assist you? Can he even speak any Latin?"

"Oh yes, my Lustia has been teaching him."

"Well, young man, show us what you can do. Say something in Latin."

Thomakin saw that he was being addressed, but had no idea what was being said. But Lustia whispered something in his ear and rescued him.

"Amo, amo, amo," he began to repeat over and over, tentatively at first but with more and more gusto as he got into the swing of things.

The assembled merchants stood open-mouthed, before bursting out in howls of laughter.

"I say, old chap, what has your daughter really been teaching the gorilla?" one of them shouted.

"Looks very much like your little Brutus is out of luck, Clavius" another added.

Lustia treated each of the mocking merchants to her best withering glare and they immediately withered. "I assume you all will have organised the obligatory welcoming Bacchanalia. Where is it to be held?" she addressed the assembly

The one known as Clavius pointed in the direction of a large villa.

"Good, let's go party!" And, so saying, Lustia grabbed Thomakin with one arm and her father with the other and marched off in the indicated direction.

14 VERCINGETORIX

Thomakin awoke with heavy hammers thudding in his head. He lifted his dazed eyes through the grey morning-after fog and discerned the murky outline of a tall figure standing over him. As he focused, the vison solidified into the unmistakable shape of Lustia. She was wearing a contended smile and not much else. He could recall nothing of the Bacchanalian revels of the evening before. A few flashes of enormous beakers of red wine drifted in and out of his consciousness. Beakers exactly like the one Lustia now held in her hand.

What had he done last night? He wished he could remember, but nothing came back to him. Had he compromised himself? "Where be I?" he asked.

"In my bed," Lustia answered. Thomakin groaned inwardly.

"How did I get here?" It was one of those reluctant questions to which the enquirer fears the answer.

"Clavius's sons carried you to this room and threw you in there. On my instructions."

"Did I...? Was there any...?"

"You were sleeping when you got here and have been in the same state until a moment ago."

"So nothing happened that you... or I...have need to regret?"

"Nothing happened. Regrets are another matter. But drink this." She handed him the glass she was holding.

The smell and sight of the red wine it contained jogged his memory. "No, not that. That's what got me here."

"And it will cure you too. And you need to be cured for we have an important appointment later this morning. You are required to help us at a meeting with the Gaul, Vercingetorix."

She forced the wine on him and he drank it. It did make him feel better – a little. "Help you how?"

"As a sort of translator."

"But I don't speak the language of this land."

"You Barbarians all speak the same. Well, pretty much. You'll manage."

The delegation that arrived at the Gaul's encampment later that day included not only Thomakin, Tiberius and Clavius with some of his friends. Lustia had dragged herself along too. She had grasped Thomakin by the arm and clung on to him for the whole journey, claiming the terrain was rough and she needed support. They were met by a guard of painted warriors with wild whoops and a threatening demeaner, but Lustia's seductive smile calmed them down. "Take us to your leader," she asked, sweetly. Saying something that was presumably the Gallic equivalent of *Come this way please*, they led the party into the presence of the great warrior leader.

"Oh, it's you lot again," he said when they were presented to him. "What are you after now?"

Thomakin translated. Lustia had been right. The languages were very similar, and although he could not understand very word, he picked up the gist of what the fearsome Gaul was saying pretty well.

"Tell him we are here to trade," Clavius said, in Latin. "And point out that we have his best interests at heart, and that trading with us can only be beneficial to him."

Lustia translated for Thomakin, who repeated it to the Gaul with the appropriate grammar and vocabulary corrections. Some of the sense of the message must have been lost in translation, for Vercingetorix replied, "Oh, here to rip me off again, as usual."

Lustia herself picked up the sense of this communication, for she spoke directly to the Gaul, "Ah, the great one likes his little joke, does he not?"

Vercingetorix's attention was addressed towards the young lady who had just spoken, and his piercing eyes inspected her from head to toe, and back up again. He must have liked what he saw, for he grinned broadly. "And who are you?" he said, leering.

Thomakin noticed this and it did not please him. He detected danger in the lustful look to which Lustia was being subjected. He was her protector, he had made a promise and there was no question of him reneging on such a solemn commitment. "She be Lustia, and she be under my protection," he told the Gaul.

"And who are you then?" Vercingetorix said, turning to the Briton.

Tiberius stepped forward. "He is my assistant and bodyguard, a formidable young man from over the water in Britain, and an expert on all aspects of combat."

"A bit of a fighter then?" the Gaul asked. The Roman deemed his question rhetorical and did not deign to answer. Before the conversation could proceed further, the burly bearded adolescent standing at the shoulder of the leader of the Gauls leaned over and whispered in the older man's ear. Both of them stared at Lustia for a few moments, and Vercingetorix nodded. "My son has indicated that he wishes to take this Lustia as his woman. How much do you want for her?"

As a suddenly pale-faced Lustia looked on, her father spoke up. "She's not for sale. She's my daughter."

"Oh, come on. You Romans will buy and sell anything to make a few sesterci. Hand her over, we'll pay a fair price."

"She is priceless, sir. You cannot have her at any price. Unless she herself is enticed by the prospect of becoming your daughter-in-law," Tiberius said.

"Well, how about it, young Lustia? My son's set his heart on you, so how does the prospect of joining yourself to a noble Gallic family grab you? It's an offer you won't get every day."

"Nothing could be further from my desires, sir," Lustia replied coldly.

"Well now, that's an awful shame, so it is. For I am one of those Dads who cannot refuse their children anything, and if I can't buy you, I'm just going to take you."

At this, young Thomakin placed his hand on his still sheathed sword, and cried. "It will not be. If you want the young lady, you'll have to kill me first. And it will not be an easy task, I swear."

Vercingetorix grinned again, and turned to his son. "Well, my lad, if you want the woman looks like you'll have to fight for her. Are you up for it, P'titorix?"

"You bet your sweet life I am, Daddy. I'll wipe the floor with this foreign upstart in no time at all."

Both of the boys drew their swords and combat commenced. It did not last long, for the young Gaul's ambitions far outmatched his abilities, while Tiberius's claims for Thomakin had been, if anything, understated. There had hardly been enough time for the Romans and the Gauls to lay their bets on their respective champions when P'titorix was forced the ground with the point of Thomakin's sword against this throat. "Yield, Gaul," the victor cried, "and renounce your claims on the young lady, if you wish to live." P'titorix promptly yielded and declared that he had no further interest in Lustia, and intended to find a bride from among his compatriots.

"You were well beaten there, son," Vercingetorix laughed. "Looks like you could do with a few lessons. Are you Romans hanging around for a while yet, by any chance."

"I will be remaining here for three weeks to complete my trade with your fellow-countrymen, but then Lustia, Thomakin and myself will leave for Rome, for we have important business to transact there."

"Three weeks. It's not bad, although more would have been better. I'll give you a contract for your assistant Thomakin to spend those three weeks undertaking the training of my men in combat skills. Agreed, Roman?"

"In principle, but it depends on the price," Tiberius answered. Negotiations began, an accord was reached, and Thomakin began his work. It was a great success for everyone. Vercingetorix felt his men were more able to defeat the hated Julius, whenever the hated enemy came back from his holiday in Rome. P'titorix soon got over his disappointment at losing Lustia, and was more confident that he would be successful if the had to fight for the next one that came along. Tiberius won on two counts: he had obtained a good price on the training contract and was so much in favour with the Gauls that he was able to trade on very favourable terms. Thomakin's affable nature made him very popular with his trainees and the valuable experience he gained in leading a group of warriors would stand him in good stead in his later career. As for Lustia, no one could be better pleased than she was. For not only had she been saved from the clutches of a gormless Gaul, but her champion had proved loyal and faithful and well up to the task. He would do for her : no need for her to look elsewhere.

15 ROME

As we worked in the Rome Antiquity Centre library,
My colleague Joanie and I saw that Livy's manuscript
had nothing to say about the journey of Thomakin
and his employers from Western Gaul to Rome. This
caused some speculation between us. I wondered if
they had perhaps travelled by the more difficult but
shorter route overland; or had they chosen the easier
but longer route by sea? Joanie frostily informed me
that that particular topic was of no interest to her,
what concerned her was what that avaricious hussy
Lustia had been doing to her beloved hero during the
journey. I pointed out that she must have devoted a lot
of time to his Latin lessons, because it appears that, on
his arrival in Rome, Thomakin had been able to
converse with everyone he met in Rome without
problems. I was awarded with an icy glare and the
assertion that I really understood nothing about the
female sex, and I could see that discretion dictated that

I did not contradict her. So instead I invited her to rejoin me in delving deeper into the Latin writings and discovering the next steps in Thomakin's great adventure.

Thomakin had been overawed by his first visit to the great city, as you might expect of an unsophisticated peasant from a savage land. So many buildings, so many streets, so many people; he had never seen anything like it, not in Britain and not even in Gaul. He was speechless, but it didn't matter, for Lustia was blabbing on and doing more than enough talking for both of them.

"Look, there's an aqueduct. It brings water from the hills into the city. It's a mark of civilisation; you don't have any of them in your barbarian country, do you?"

She didn't wait for an answer, and Thomakin realised this was one of those conversations in which he was not required to participate. Something else had grabbed her attention, and she continued on without taking breath.

"And that's the Temple of Jupiter, where real Roman priests officiate. Compare that to those dowdy hillocks your barbaric Druids worship on. And over there's the Bathhouse. I expect Daddy will be taking you there to clean up before he presents you to anyone. And that area of the city is the Forum, where the rulers of the city meet to arrange affairs of state. It's a pity there are so many plebeians about, or you could see it a lot better and admire."

"Plebeians?" Thomakin was keen to show he was listening to her.

"The common people. The riff-raff. They're not important. We patricians are the ones who run the city, and indeed all the Roman territories."

"So they're the lowest of the low. Just like me, I suppose."

"Oh no, they're a lot better than you, barbarian. At least they're Roman Citizens. Savages like you are less than nothing."

Thomakin smiled. Social status was not a big thing for him. "So the likes of me are bottom of the pile, then?"

"If you're some kind of inverted snob, I'm sorry to disappoint you, for at least you're a freeman. The slaves are a long way below you."

"And I suppose when the slaves get frustrated, they kick the dogs?"

"Our own slaves never get frustrated. Daddy treats them well. They are like family members…almost."

At this point Tiberius, who was already far in front of them, shouted back at them. "Come on you two, hurry up. You can show Thomakin the sights tomorrow, daughter. The slaves will have taken our luggage to the villa and have our food ready. We must not disappoint them."

"See, I told you. Daddy has the greatest respect for his slaves." Lustia grabbed Thomakin by the hand and dragged him after her father.

Thomakin was no less impressed by the family villa than he had been by the city. It was enormous, much bigger than the one Tiberius had in Britain and any he had seen among the merchants in Gaul. The beauty of the decoration dazzled him: the ornate fountains, the mosaic scenes on the tiled floors and walls, and the beautiful craftsmanship in the furniture, which particularly impressed him, for it evoked in him a small twinge of nostalgia for his own achievements in crafting ornamental boots. He turned to Lustia, who seemed as awed by the splendour as he was. "How could you ever have left this palace for our land?" he asked her. "The memories of it must have haunted you constantly."

"I don't remember it. Daddy took me off to your savage lands while I was still a child. All I know about Rome I learned from books and visiting merchants."

"But now you have seen it as a grown up, surely you will never leave it. You'll find some nice patrician like yourself to marry and live here in luxury for the rest of your life."

This optimist proposition did not produce the expected response from the young lady. "Don't tell me what I will do with my life, Barbarian. And don't expect to get out of your responsibilities to me so easily."

Before Thomakin could formulate an acceptable apology for having upset her, Tiberius called out. "I'm sorry, daughter, but after lunch I have to deprive you of the company of your friend, for he and I must go to the baths and clean up after the journey. And afterwards, we go to the Forum, for I have business to transact and Thomakin has a lot to learn here in Rome, and we must start at once."

"Take him, Daddy. Take him now. For he seems to be determined to annoy me today."

"Oh, that doesn't sound like our Thomakin. A gentler and more affable person does not exist. He would only have your best interests at heart."

"Daddy, what can you imagine a savage like him could know about my best interests? Take him away before he upsets me even more."

"We will be gone soon enough, but first we must eat. Come and let us enjoy the delights the slaves have prepared for us."

"As you wish, father, but tell the Barbarian to keep silent during the meal. I have had quite enough of his incessant and inappropriate chatter today."

They proceeded to the triclinium and were served a sumptuous repast with meats, fruits and fine wine. Conversation was lacking, for Tiberius and Thomakin were men of few words and Lustia was preoccupied with staring at the young Briton, hoping to see signs of remorse at his unwanted words earlier. Thomakin was as inscrutable as ever. By the time he and her father finally left for the bathhouse, Lustia had decided that Thomakin still needed more work if she was to get him right.

16 THE INVASION PLAN

Refreshed by the hot and cold plunges and by the energetic pummelling of the masseur, a freshly be-togaed Thomakin and his employer left the bathhouse and made their way along the Roman streets to what seemed to him to be the main square of the city. From time to time the older man would be greeted by a *Salve Tiberii* and he would respond by a nod, or, less frequently, a wave and a smile.

"You seem to know a lot of people here, father Tiberius?" Thomakin ventured.

"Rogues and scoundrels, most of them, my boy. You need to learn who to trust. We are in a city of intrigue and corruption and too many of our citizens are devious and duplicitous."

Thomakin was reminded of how the treacherous Beaufox had had him exiled, and reflected that perhaps there was no great difference between savagery and civilisation.

They entered a magnificent building, which surpassed even the opulence that Thomakin was beginning to get used to. His low whistle of appreciation seemed to encourage his employer.

"The Curia Hostilia, Thomakin," Tiberius explained. Then, with an exaggerated wave that was to become the standard gesture of tourist guides everywhere, he continued. "And here we have the renowned Tabula Valeria, which depicts the victory of Manius Valerius Maximus Corvinus Messalla over Hiero and the Carthaginians nearly three hundred years ago." But for Thomakin the real life going on inside the building was more interesting than a painting on a wall.

Small groups of noblemen were scattered all around, whispering in each others ears and nodding agreement with false smiles. At one end, the largest group was dominated by one tall fellow, nose high in the air, who was graciously accepting the fawning supplications of his companions. His attention was diverted from the torrent of praise by the arrival of the merchant and his aide. The look of disdain he had been wearing was replaced by a broad grin, and, pushing his entourage out of the way, he made a beeline for the newcomers. "Tibby, old boy, how are you doing?"

Tiberius shook his hand as he answered. "Julesy, what a surprise. I had thought you'd be back in Gaul now."

"Got to look after my own interests here, old chap. Vanquishing the whole Gallic army is child's play compared to watching your back in this den of snakes."

"Talking of Vercingetorix's lot, I came across him while I was in Gaul on the way here."

"Good to know that. You wouldn't have any intelligence on the rebellious savage that might help me sort him out when I go back, would you?"

"Well, I can tell you that he hired my organisation to give his troops a bit of training. Lucrative contract, it was too."

"I hope you didn't train them too well. But then, you've never been a soldier. What could you teach them?"

"Just basic man-to-man fighting skills."

"No strategy?"

"No tactics or strategy."

"Well that's OK then. They'll still be disorganised and clueless. If they're a little bit better with the sword and shield they'll just make it all the more interesting for our boys. But what do you know about hand-to-hand combat, Tibby?"

"Oh it wasn't me, Julesy. The training was done by my new assistant here, Thomakin the Briton. And a damn fine fighter he is too, I can tell you."

Julius Caesar, for that was indeed who Tiberius was talking to, paused for a moment. "Hmmmm… Briton, you say?"

"And an exemplary member of his race too, Julesy."

"It was just that I was thinking that, you know, after polishing off the Gauls, I might nip over there and help myself to bit of booty. The young man wouldn't be interested in a well-paid position as a spy for me, by any chance?"

Tiberius frowned, and shook his finger at his friend. "Now, now, Julesy, that's not how it's done. Thomakin works for me, and if you want to utilise his services you'll need to sign a contract with my firm. And it had better be a good one; our services don't come cheap."

"What about 30% of the profit on all my loot; and I'll make sure my soldiers sell anything they capture personally to you at a really good price. You'll make a fortune."

"Not very attractive, Julesy. Can't you do better?"

"Tell you what, old boy, I'll throw in 50% on the sale of all the slaves we capture. How about that?"

At this point, Thomakin pulled his employer a few steps away from the great general. "No slaves," he whispered in his boss's ear.

"It's good money," Tiberius whispered back.

"I'm not going to help you Romans sell my countrymen into bondage."

"Yes, well maybe you're right."

Caesar, being unable to catch the sense of this conversation, interrupted tetchily. "What's the savage saying?"

"Julesy, to tell the truth, we're not sure the slave thing is a great idea."

"But we always take slaves, Tibby. It's a custom."

"We think it might be counter-productive in this campaign. You see, unlike the Carthaginians and the Iberians, they're not used to the concept of slave-taking. In fact, they're even more opposed to it than the Gauls, and look at the problems you're having with them."

"But it's the slavery thing makes campaigns cost-effective. We don't go into these wars just for fun, you know."

"If you'll forgive me saying so, that's a very short-term view. I've got a better suggestion, if you're ready to listen."

"Go ahead, Tibby. You know I've always trusted your commercial judgement."

"Look, Thomakin here is not only a great warrior, but he's a real people person. He very quickly has everyone he meets eating out of his hand. Now, if you were to give me an exclusive contract for British trade, and we went over there with Thomakin and a little expeditionary force, I'm sure we could soon establish him as the leader of all Britain, and he would get all the tribes to cooperate with us. We'd split the profits fifty-fifty with you. You'd make a lot more than from a quick and troublesome invasion of a hostile territory. What do you think?"

"Hmm…has possibilities."

"Let me put it this way. It would be at no risk to you. I'd fund everything and arrange for Thomakin here to get a bit of military training on battlefield tactics and commanding an army. He'll be here in Rome for the next couple of years learning the business, so he'll have plenty to time to fit it in. And you won't have to waste your time in savage territory; as soon as you've conquered the Gauls you could come straight back here and look after your political interests. I wouldn't want to leave that Cassius without being able to keep an eye on him, if I were you."

"Lean and hungry look, you mean."

"Exactly. Well, are you up for it?"

"I am. Come over tomorrow and we'll thrash out the details."

The next day, the necessary arrangements were made and the appropriate contracts signed. Thomakin began his two-year training in how to become a warrior merchant and future ruler, and settled into a life of luxury in Rome, safely enveloped in the constant attentions and protection of the determined Lustia.

17 A LOVE STORY

At this time, I was working harder than I had ever done in my life before. I was spending my days in the library of the Roman Antiquity Centre with Joanie translating the recently discovered account of Thomakin Kobbler's adventures. At night, I toiled over the Stonehenge Stones, catching up on what Beaufox Headman was up to while his arch rival was gallivanting all over Europe. As if this wasn't enough, I had to devote the early evening to keeping my friend Joanie amused by taking her to dine and either discussing what we had learned that day or updating her on the events in Beaufox's Britain. It was while I was doing the latter and relaying the story below to her that something occurred that would result in a major change in the circumstances of my life.

In spite of her youth, Innocenta Kobbler was a young lady of remarkable determination. Her real name was Thelma, which to her sounded too much like the hammer thudding the nails into the boots she made. So she had herself the chosen the unusual name Innocenta, and for a good reason. Less than a couple of years younger than her long-exiled cousin, she had heard of his vow of monogamy and had decided that she too would subscribe to this philosophy. She scorned the enticements of the village boys and ignored the goading of the girls. No, she was resolved to keep herself pure for her chosen one, to whom she would remain faithful to for ever once she had secured him, for her intended victim was as yet unaware of his fate.

She realised that her choice for her true love came with advantages and disadvantages. The principal advantage was that her chosen one also subscribed to monogamy, as his whole family had done for generations. The major disadvantage was that he was not only one of the hated Headmans, but indeed the most hated of that clan, for she had indeed set her sights on the detested Beaufox Headman, the chieftain of the settlement. No one in the village really trusted Beaufox, and they were all terrified of him, and not without cause. He ruled by cunning and cruelty, and suspicions abounded as to how accidental the accidental demise of his father and elder brother had really been. But these flaws and rumours were as nothing to a heart consumed by love.

Nor could one say that physical attraction played a great role in Innocenta's infatuation. She was a tall willowy girl, fair of face and could have had her choice of the eligible male population. The object of her affection was small and spindly; while one could not say he was malformed, he was certainly not well formed. Love indeed is blind. So blind, in fact, that she was determined that he would be hers, no matter the consequences.

But there was an obstacle in the way of Innocenta's romantic strategy. How was she to secure him? The Headman's were notorious for their assiduous practice of intermarriage, so she needed some way to overcome this. Then there was the business of getting him to notice her. Although she personally did not adhere to the social conventions of the village, he almost certainly did. And, according to these conventions, she was so far socially inferior to the object of her infatuation that it was likely that, even if she stood on top of him, he was hardly likely to notice. Determined as she was, it seemed a hopeless case.

But, unknown to Innocenta, it was perhaps not so hopeless. For Beaufox had indeed noticed her; in fact, he was as consumed by love for her as she was for him. Unfortunately, Beaufox's romantic aspirations also faced a seemingly unsurmountable obstacle. It wasn't the inter-marriage thing; Beaufox had long since become aware of the effects of a limited gene pool on his family's health, and had decided to discontinue the practice. Nor was it timidity – exactly. Wasn't he determined and ruthless enough to get whatever he wanted, and didn't he have two faithful lieutenants who would do his bidding to fulfil his every desire?

But affair of the heart are different from other aspects of life and the one thing that Beaufox feared more than anything was to be the victim of unrequited love. Of course, if he wanted Innocenta, all he had to do was go down to the Kobbler hovel and take her. The trouble was, he wanted *her* to want *him*, and he was so riven with the fear of a refusal that he just could not bring himself to ask her.

So the great romance was stuck in an impasse with no way out. Two lost souls, each longing for the other but without a way to communicate their longing. Star-crossed lovers indeed!

Then, tormented by that unsatisfied gnawing, Beaufox finally decided to act. Perhaps if he had Innocenta constantly by his side, some magic would happen and she would be his at last. He summonsed Cathbad the Druid.

"I have a task for you, priest. I've had enough of the incessant gossip between my mother and sister over dinner every evening. From now on I'm going to be dining alone. So I will need to recruit a serving wench to look after me."

"Did you have anyone in mind?"

"Well, obviously she has to be easy on the eye, an ugly one would be as bad as sharing a table with my annoying family. There's that little Kobbler girl who's quite presentable. What's her name? Innocenta, I believe. What about her?"

"Oh, I don't think the Kobblers would allow that. They're very proud of their family artisanship, you know…" Cathbad had meant to go on with his explanation, but the dark and violent glare from Beaufox stopped him in his tracks. "Of course, I'll see to it, sir."

"Of course you will. Right away." Beaufox waved his hand in dismissal and the old priest trundled off.

Cathbad had been right. When he broached the recruitment of their most attractive young woman to wait on the despicable leader of the Headmans, the Kobbler clan were up in arms.

"No, no, no. We'll not be sacrificing our little Innocenta to that brute," said her father. "Over my dead body."

"Well, it might be," answered Cathbad. "You know what Beaufox is like?"

"Let him try, our friends the Armours will be with us on this."

"I wouldn't count on it. The great one is all powerful."

"Besides, Innocenta is an artisan, an artist even. Nobody has made boots like she can, not since Thomakin was banished. She won't be wasting that talent by becoming a serving girl to Beaufox," her mother said.

"Or whatever else that devious rogue wants with her," her father added. "We'll stop him in his tracks, won't we boys?"

Loud jeers of agreement rose from the assembled Kobbler ranks.

But Innocenta had been lurking on the side-lines, and she saw her chance. If she could be constantly close to her beloved, anything could happen. She shouted above the hubbub. "I don't mind doing it. I'll sacrifice myself for the safety of my friends and family." She was a devious one, that one.

The Kobblers, in unison, began to entreat her not to put her head in the jaws of the avaricious and treacherous lion, but she paid them no heed. She had already grabbed Cathbad's hand and was leading him away in the general direction of the Headmans' section of the settlement.

18 THE CRAFTY BRIDE

Innocenta decided Cathbad was walking too slowly, so she released his hand from her grasp and marched on with determination to the Headman dwelling. She passed the mysterious and enormous new building that Beaufox was having constructed and swept into the lair Beaufox shared with his mother and his remaining siblings.

Beaufox was so surprised to see her striding in boldly that he was speechless. He had expected that she would have shuffled into his presence reluctantly, clinging unwillingly to Cathbad's overpowering arm.

"What's all this about, Headman?" she shouted, folding her arms and fixing him with a glare usually reserved for the naughty children of the family. If she had been anyone else, he would not have put up with such an attitude, but in Innocenta he found it quite endearing. Such is the nature of infatuation. "Well, have you lost your voice?" she insisted when he didn't answer.

"Er, I'm looking for a girl to serve me, and I thought you would fit perfectly," he managed to utter.

"Serve you? What kind of service are you looking for? Do not imagine I am one of those flighty promiscuous girls of the village. I am resolved to remain pure until I find the true love of my life."

" Very commendable. But let me assure you no impropriety is involved, Miss Innocenta."

Innocenta felt a wave of disappointment. A little bit of impropriety was what she had been hoping for. Perhaps she had overplayed the 'hard-to- get' card a little bit. "And is this position residential, or do I have to struggle up from the far reaches of the village every day, Lord Beaufox?" The 'Lord Beaufox' was an attempt to appear more deferential, and she hoped she hadn't overdone it. The smile on Beaufox's face suggested she maybe had.

"Oh residential, of course. I would not impose a daily commute upon you."

'Residential' was promising. But she didn't want to seem to eager, so she looked around the Headman roundhouse and affected disdain. "This place seems to me overcrowded as it is, do you have room for another one?"

"But you will not be living here. You and I will be ensconced in the new house next door, which will from henceforth will be called 'The Palace'.

So that's what that enormous new building was for. Beaufox was moving out of the family home to wallow in luxury. He was looking more and more like a good catch, if she could reel him in. "In that enormous building, just you and I?"

"You will have your own space," he answered, and as her eyes widened, he added, "which will be discretely curtained off, of course?"

"Will there be no other servants, then?" she asked.

"Would we have need of other servants?"

"A cook?"

"You can't cook?"

"Of course I can cook, but wouldn't it be a bit much for me to cook and serve at the same time?"

Beaufox paused before answering, and his brows furrowed. Innocenta could see she had raised a problem he hadn't thought of. "Miss Innocenta, I have a confession to make. You see, I am not happy in large crowds, and while I believe that the pair of us together would be idyllic, the presence of even one other would be very stressful for me. I am more than happy to wait a little longer for my meals in order to avoid that stress."

"In that case, sir, I will reciprocate your gesture by assuming the more onerous task of both cooking and serving with the aim of facilitating a calm state of mind in your lordship."

The bargain was thus concluded and Beaufox and Innocenta moved into the best house in the settlement. This, of course, produced the expected rumours among the populace, whose imagination would not stretch to envisaging a young feisty couple together day and night and maintaining relations on a strictly platonic level. The many gifts of jewellery and clothing that Beaufox bestowed on his new servant only served to fuel the fire of gossip.

But, to the eternal regret of both participants in this unconventional relationship, these rumours were entirely without foundation. On an intellectual level, the pair grew very close. Innocenta comforted him when the affairs of state were bringing him down, and indeed she was often able to contribute useful suggestions to help him achieve his ends. He was amazed that he been so lucky to find a soulmate as devious as himself, who would support him in all his endeavours, and never bring up disturbing questions about the morality of what he was doing. With Innocenta by his side, Beaufox prospered, and to a lesser extent the village prospered too, although of course not as much as its leader did. But a cloud of sadness and dissatisfaction hovered above the young couple.

Despite Innocenta's tacit encouragement, Beaufox seemed unable to read the signals, and his fear of rejection was still hindering his romantic aspirations. On her part, Innocenta was restrained from a more overt seduction by her need to be sure of his eternal faithfulness. One of them needed to take action to break out of the impasse, and it fell to Innocenta to make the first move.

The opportunity came when Beaufox came home one evening, his face drawn and his hands trembling.

"Rough day, dear?" Innocenta asked. Their relationship had at least proceeded to these innocuous terms of endearment.

"My mother's been nagging me again, my little one. Telling me how the whole village disapproves of us living together and exhorting me to kick you out and tie up with one of my eligible cousins or second cousins. It drives me crazy."

"Sit down, sweetheart, and let me massage your temples. That will soothe you."

"Oh, yes please," said Beaufox. It was an offer he had never had before.

Innocenta set to work, her long deft fingers gliding over the skin of his forehead. She could see he was enjoying the experience. Emboldened by his initial positive reaction to her offer, and his subsequent sighs of pleasure, Innocenta decided now was the time. "Close your eyes and form your mouth into the shape of the letter 'O'," she instructed.

Beaufox did so, and Innocenta planted a kiss on his receptive mouth. A long lingering kiss, which led to further intimacies that very night. The barrier had been breached.

Henceforth, happiness reigned in Beaufox's Palace. Cathbad pronounced an edict that the gods had decreed that the couple would now be known as Lord Beaufox and Lady Innocenta, and in very short order a couple of heirs were produced and the succession of the royal lineage ensured.

I was somewhat surprised by Joanie's reaction when I related this latest episode in the Story of the Stones to her. I had expected her usual diatribe against the scheming Beaufox, the sycophantic Cathbad and his whole Druid religion. But instead her eyes had glazed over and a distracted grin had taken possession of her face. "Close your eyes and form your mouth into the shape of the letter 'O'," she said to me. Not wishing to cause offence, I did as I was told, and quickly found her lips pressed against mine as she whispered, "Jamie, oh Jamie, my Jamie." I was a tad taken aback, but it wasn't an unpleasant experience, although unexpected. I had always believed our relationship was strictly professional. I shall move in with you and we shall move on to the next stage. Right away, this very evening. What do you think?"

Although it came completely out of the blue, I only needed a few seconds to consider the offer. It made perfect sense. The expenses of our research were becoming somewhat overwhelming, and her suggestion would mean that we could hire one hotel room instead of two. And I could give up my rather dingy and expensive flat back home, and move into the well appointed house she had inherited from her parents. And, of course, there were the side benefits, such as I had just experienced. "Good idea," I said.

And that is how my relationship with my esteemed colleague moved onto a more intimate basis.

19 REJECTED PROPOSALS

Livy's previously undiscovered manuscript shed little light on the commercial and military training Thomakin received while in Rome. It mentions, with no details, that he visited the far reaches of the Roman Empire on his employer's business. We can only presume that it was on these trips that he became acquainted with the ploys and practices of the Tiberian business empire. As for his military training, Livy merely announces that, under the guidance of the great Pompey, he was schooled in all the latest Roman battle practices. Joanie, with whom I was by now on more intimate terms, suggested that these would not prove too useful when he was at the head of a bunch of uncouth and untrained Britons, and I have to say I concurred with this rather insightful deduction on her part.

However, one event is described in detail in the Livian writings. We can only suppose it is included because it involves a personage of some historical note who would later pay a pivotal role in the future of the Roman state. As it also had a major bearing on the future career of our brave Thomakin, I will recount it in some detail here.

While Tiberius was trailing Thomakin everywhere on their frequent trips to far-flung lands, his beautiful and eligible daughter was not left to languish. The illustrious senator Brutus, a friend of both 'Julesy' Caesar and the young lady's father, had decided to save Lustia from boredom and take under his wing. He introduced her into his social circle. This decision was not entirely philanthropic, for the senator was possessed of a son of marriageable age whom he was having difficulty getting rid of. This spindly, spotty lad, known as Gentilus, was in every way the contrast to his father. Brutus strode; Gentilus minced. The voice of Brutus beamed; that of Gentilus squeaked like a mouse. It was said in society that 'there was a bit to much of the Greek' about him. Frankly, he did look somewhat effeminate, and his lack of any interaction with the opposite sex seemed to confirm the rumours, although who knew if he deliberately avoided girls or girls just avoided him. In any case, Lustia often found herself in Bacchanalian celebrations, seated beside the spotty youth and being subjected to his incessant toothy grin.

When they were in Rome, Brutus also invited Tiberius and his young assistant to these revels, taking care to position Thomakin as far away as possible from his son and Lustia. He realised that Gentilus was no competition for the Briton when to came to the affections of young ladies. On these occasions, Thomakin saw from afar the long languid looks being bestowed on his employer's daughter by the son of their host. He also noted that the young woman's response to this attention was total indifference, and though it may have been a veneer, at heart he felt she really just didn't fancy him much.

When, one day, Gentilus turned up at the Tiberian villa, enquiring after Thomakin, the Briton was puzzled. What could the puny patrician want with him? The rumours surrounding the senator's son's sexuality were discussed freely among the young Romans with whom Thomakin shared his military training, so it was with some trepidation that he agreed that Gentilus should be admitted into his presence.

"Thomakin the Briton?" the boy asked when the slave ushered him into the atrium.

"I be he. And you be Gentilus, I presume?"

"Indeed I am, sir, and I need to have words with you."

"It be my pleasure, go ahead."

"I am here to challenge you to gladiatorial combat."

"What? You… against me?"

"Exactly, Mr Thomakin. Swords and shields, in the true military manner."

"For what reason? Have I offended you in some way? If so, I be sorry, for I did not do it intentionally."

"It is required of me by your employer's daughter, the lovely Lustia."

"Please excuse me, but I do not understand. Would you care to elucidate further, Gentilus?"

"When I swore my undying love for the young lady, she informed that there was an impediment, and it could not be. You were sworn to be her protector, to save her from all threats, and no man could approach her while you lived. So my case was hopeless, unless I could arrange for your demise in free and fair competition. She suggested a gladiatorial encounter, to the death in the true and respected Roman tradition, would be an acceptable solution,."

"Did she indeed?" Thomakin turned to the slave, who, sensing a bit of entertainment was in the offing, had hung around to observe. "Go and fetch your mistress at once, for we have a problem here to resolve. And do not inform her of the presence of this young man."

Sensing more fun was afoot, the slave ran off, grinning broadly. He returned a few moments later with Lustia in tow.

"You wanted to talk to me, Thomakin?" Then she spied the young Roman. "Oh, it's you, Gentilus. What are you doing here?"

"You know very well what he be doing here, because he came at your behest. What's all this nonsense you have been telling him about you and me? Why did you ask him to fight me?"

"Well, you are my protector, are you not?"

"Only from danger or unwanted attention. Not from genuine proposals. Look at the boy, you know he has no chance in combat against me. You'd be sending him to a certain death."

"It would prove his attachment to me."

"Posthumously. Don't use me to get rid of your unwanted suitors. If you don't like him, show some courage and tell him directly."

Lustia turned to the young Roman. "I don't like you, Gentilus," she announced in a firm voice.

Tears welled up in the Roman's eyes and he began to visibly tremble. "The shame," he squealed. "The shame of being rejected by you, you... heartless hussy. That's it, I am finished with woman. From now on, I will live celibate for the rest of my life and Daddy can look elsewhere for someone to provide him with an heir. Goodbye, O' cruel temptress. Goodbye for ever." And he swept from the villa, leaving Lustia and Thomakin standing open-mouthed, and the slave quietly sniggering into his sleeve.

"I though you were a bit hard on him, Lustia," Thomakin said, once Gentilus had gone.

"You told me to tell him if I didn't like him, so I told him."

"You might have been more tactful."

"No, no more tact. I've had enough of this prevaricating. I'm just going to say what I'm going to say. Sit down, Thomakin."

Thomakin sat on the edge of one of the benches. Lustia knelt beside him and took his hands in hers.

"Look me in the eyes, Thomakin."

"Why? What's the matter with your eyes?"

"Nothing. Now don't talk, just listen."

Thomakin closed his wide-open mouth and looked at her. She had a strange wild expression on her face.

"You know that you and I are looking for the right one?" she began.

Thomakin opened his mouth to reply, but then he remembered her rules for the game and just nodded.

"Well, I've found mine," she went on.

Thomakin was somewhat taken aback at this news. He realised he wasn't quite ready to part with her just yet. But if she had settled on some young Roman, he would be happy for her. And it meant he would have a bit more freedom for his own projects, didn't it? Just as well, maybe. "My congratulations. I hope he be worthy of you. But he must be, or I'm sure you wouldn't have chosen him."

"Oh, he is," Lustia confirmed.

"And you won't be needing my protection now, will you?"

Lustia squeezed his hand. "You silly man. The 'one' … 'it'… 'he' if you like, is you."

Thomakin pulled his hands free and raised them to his face. "Me? There must be some mistake."

"No mistake, Thomakin." Thomakin was speechless. Lustia grabbed his hands back and fixed her eyes on his. "Don't tell me you don't feel anything for me, here." She pulled his hands to her heart.

Thomakin allowed a squeal to escape and grabbed back possession of his stolen appendages before they were taken somewhere they shouldn't be going.

"You do have feelings, don't you?" she insisted.

"Well, yes…but…"

"But what?"

"You know, I be still young. And I need to be sure of my feelings. I made a sacred vow to be faithful. What if I took someone and she wasn't just right? It would be a disaster."

Lustia sniffed. "You mean, you're not prepared to take me?"

Thomakin stuttered. "No…no…n.n.n.not exactly. I'm just not ready to take you yet, that's all."

Lustia stood up and placed her hands firmly on her hips. "And I'm supposed to hang around waiting until you make up your mind?"

Thomakin hung his head. If there was a suitable response to that question, he had no idea what it was.

Lustia exploded. "Listen, you savage barbarian, you just don't know what you want. Let me tell you, you're the one for me and I'm the one for you. When it finally dawns on you, I'll be here wating for you. You'd just better have a good apology at the ready."

Lustia swept out of the room, leaving poor Thomakin to contemplate his inevitable fate.

20 ROMANCE IN ROME

Both of our historical sources talk about Thomakin's departure for Rome and his arrival back in Britain. Livy describes in some detail the nuptial celebrations of Thomakin and Lustia before they embark on one of Tiberius's merchant vessels for the Briton's homeland. The etchings on the Stones from Wiltshire mention that when the future King Thomakin arrived back in the country from his sojourn in foreign lands, he brought with him his beautiful lady who would become his Queen. And while the Stones detail the rise of Thomakin to the heady heights of ruler of all the lands of the Britons, Livy notes that 'Thomakin arrived in Britain and began to win over the whole populace to his rule, persuading them to accept free trade with the Romans.' Joanie and I, as serious historians, took considerable satisfaction that these two independent and unconnected sources corroborated each other, for such corroboration convinces the academic world that we are dealing here with fact and not legend.

Livy's account states that 'no man can resist indefinitely the wishes and desires of a determined woman,' and quotes the case of Thomakin and Lustia as an example. *(Incidentally, as we translated this quote, Joanie beamed knowingly at me and said that this was a timeless truism, as meaningful today as it was back then.)*

Lustia was relentless in her pursuit of the young Briton. Every time he returned from a trip with her father, she would corner him, and ask, "Well, did you find your chosen one on this trip, then?"

Thomakin's answer was invariable. "I did not go on the journey for such a purpose, but to help your father and learn from him."

To which Lustia replied, every time, "Ah! So you didn't find her. That's because you already have, and you're too stupid to accept it."

At other random times throughout their two years in Rome, she would find him alone in the villa and never wasted such an opportunity. "You do have some feelings for me?" she would whimper.

Thomakin would admit reluctantly that he had felt strange stirrings.

"And no other woman has produced the same effects on you, have they?"

"Not yet, but..." was his stock response, but it did not quench Lustia's desire.

"Nor ever will," she would say.

Most of the time, Thomakin refused to continue the discourse, for fear he would be drawn into a situation he was not yet quite ready for. But sometimes he would sigh, and say, "What we feel may be no more than lust, Lustia. And how disastrous it would be if we later discovered our error, and were compelled, by the love of another, to break those vows we both made of eternal monogamy. And I'm not thinking of myself, but also of you."

This always produced the same answer. "I do not need you to think for me, barbarian. I can think for myself." And she would sweep him aside with disdain, secretly hoping that he would repent his stubbornness.

Under such a determined and sustained assault, Thomakin could not resist for ever. Indeed, his lessons in military theory had taught him that victory under such an attack was unlikely, and a good soldier knows when the time comes flee to fight another day. But the bonds of duty prevented him from going anywhere, and he had no choice but to endure the relentless assault as well as he could. The end result was inevitable, but at this point Lustia did not know that.

As their imminent departure from Rome approached, her situation became more and more desperate. She had made little progress. True, she had managed to get him to admit that he was not completely devoid of feelings for her, but that was a long way from him declaring undying love. She needed a change of tack. Up to then, she had been playing on his emotions, but now she decided it was time to resort to logic.

"Thomakin, I know the new plan involves you going to Britain to become the leader of the whole country, to be installed as the very first King of Britannia."

"Something like that. But I not be doing it for myself. It be the only way to prevent your Caesar from enslaving masses of my people. And your Dad thinks it'll be good for business, as well."

"Whatever. But I've been thinking and I've come up with a problem. And also a solution. Shall I enlighten you?"

Thomakin shrugged; he knew she would anyway.

"Well, if you're going there as a King, you'll be expected to have a Queen. It's the custom."

Thomakin knew that it certainly wasn't the custom in his home country, but he allowed Lustia to carry on anyway.

"Of course, if you were to take a wife from one of the tribes, you would upset all the rest, and your hopes of uniting the nation would be dashed. Far better to arrive with a nice, pretty, personable, neutral foreign wife already in place, don't you think?"

He could see where this was going and decided to nip it in the bud. "Or perhaps, just to stay single, at least until we have completed our mission."

Lustia was not to be discouraged this easily. "No, no, no, Thomakin. That would never work. Everywhere you went, the village chieftains would be throwing their daughters at you; you wouldn't get a minute's peace. And when you rejected them, something you're very good at, it would just breed resentment and put your mission at risk. No, my ideas is a much better one, don't you agree?"

Lustia nodded sagely, secure in the belief that her argument was solid and unbeatable. But Thomakin refused the bait. "Lustia, you know my view on romantic attachments. There be no question of me allying myself to a lady in marriage of convenience merely to satisfy political aims. I be resolved to wait until Cupid blesses me with a little arrow from his bow."

Lustia stomped off, thinking that, if she had her way, instead of an arrow, he would be receiving a large spear in a place that would be exceedingly painful every time he sat down.

When her anger subsided, she returned to her plotting, but nothing came to mind. Then, with only one week of their time in Rome left, she decided that she had no choice but to risk all. Logic had failed, but her call to his emotions had at least produced an acknowledgement that he found her somewhat attractive. It was time to test the depth of his feelings. All or nothing.

Thomakin was busy all day training the motley crew of expat Britons that Tiberius had recruited for their army, and he came home each evening tired out. Lustia judged this the best time to catch him, when his defences were at their weakest. "Thomakin, I've made an important decision I need to tell you about."

Thomakin, although exhausted, was ever polite. "Yes Lustia?"

"I'm not going to come to Britain with you. If you do not want me, I will stay here in Rome and look elsewhere. Off you go across the seas, leaving behind the one who adores you. I hope you have a good time."

He took a minute to reply, before answering in a small voice. "You're really not going to come? You're going to abandon both your father and me? You can't mean it?"

"Oh, but I do. A girl can only take so much rejection, no matter how besotted she is."

"But, I am supposed to protect you. How can I do that when we are separated by hundreds of leagues?"

"Your problem, Thomakin."

"Please reconsider. What can I do to make you change your mind?"

"You know what," she replied, and left, leaving him to contemplate on how he really felt about her.

The next morning, before leaving for work, he grabbed her and asked her to marry him. According to the custom, Lustia asked him when he wanted the wedding to take place.

"Next year?" he suggested. She shook her head.

"Earlier?" She nodded.

"Next month?" She shook her head again, silently mouthing *no..no..no*.

"Next week?" he offered, but she repeated her last response.

"In days, then. In ….." She was holding up two fingers as he babbled on. "Two days," he finished, to be rewarded by a smile.

"Now you must speak to my father," she told him. "Go and find him. I will wait here"

Thomakin found Tiberius in the garden, admiring the display of colours and breathing in the soporific scent of Mediterranean flowers in full bloom.

"Ah, Thomakin, I shall miss such splendour when we go back to your homeland. I'm afraid Britain does not have the climate, or you Britons the skills, to produce such opulence. But duty calls, eh?"

"Talking about duty, father Tiberius, I have come to ask for your daughter's hand in marriage."

A sly smile broke out on the old Roman's visage. "And do you come of your own free will?"

"I think so, but we both know Lustia. She went to considerable effort to help me make up my mind."

"Forgive me for asking, but it is the custom to ensure the bridegroom has not been ensnared by devious trickery. And you have chosen the date?"

"In two days."

"Perfect. It is short notice, but, to tell the truth, Lustia has had the necessary clothing and adornment for the whole wedding party and all the guests in storage for a year now."

"Clothes for the guests as well?"

"It is the custom. Everyone must be dressed the same so the unfriendly gods cannot identify the bridal couple and inflict a curse upon them. And there is another custom that might surprise you, but I'm afraid it is necessary."

"Yes?" Thomakin replied, hesitatingly.

"You are expected to come and violently seize the bride from the arms of her parents, in this case only me. She will protest and scream, as if she is afraid and unwilling. You must not be put off by this, for it is the tradition for the young lady to pretend unwillingness."

"In Lustia's case, there could be no question of me being duped by such pretence."

"Quite so. It is well to understand your wife right from the beginning. You may now go back to your intended and tell her that everything is arranged. Although she will know that, as she arranged it all herself."

Two days later, the marriage ceremony took place, with an excess of frivolity and an even bigger excess of wine. Thomakin tried to thank the guests for attending at such short notice, only to be told time and time again that they had received their invitations six months previously. As was the Roman custom, the marriage was consummated that very evening in the large ceremonial wedding bed reserved for the purpose, an experience enjoyed to the maximum by the two young participants. By the next evening, a relieved father, a delighted daughter and a bemused son-in-law were safely installed on one of the two merchant vessels destined for Britain and their next adventure.

21 AN OFFER SCORNED

I was a little surprised by Joanie's reaction to Livy's account of Lustia's entrapment of Thomakin and their subsequent nuptials. I had become accustomed to her worship of our ancient British hero, and indeed of her overly protective instincts towards him. As a consequence, I had fully expected a tirade against the new bride, and the devious and scheming foils she had used to capture her prize. But quite the opposite was the case. "Smart woman, that Lustia" was all that she said, but the look she gave me as she spoke these words rendered me more than a little uncomfortable, I can tell you.

In any case, we had devoured all the relevant Livy writings on our British ancestor and there was no more to be learned in Rome. So, like Thomakin and Lustia, we abandoned balmy Mediterranean evenings and returned to the cold climate of our native lands. Like them, we too set up house together, for Joanie insisted that I should move in with her, and, given the strained state of my financial resources, I readily agreed. It was a pleasant as well as a convenient decision, for there is nothing to beat the pleasure to be had when, as you struggle over the intellectually exhausting task of deciphering ancient scribblings, a freshly brewed cup of tea is thrust into your tired hand, especially if it is accompanied by a favourite biscuit. In this way, our work proceeded in an atmosphere of domestic bliss.

The etchings on the stones picked up the adventures of Thomakin again as he disembarked in Britain with his new wife, his father-in-law and his army of fifty or so Roman trained British warriors. The party made its way to Tiberius's British villa, with Lustia and her father leading the way. Behind them came the soldiers, led by Thomakin, with an ex-slave called Attacus by his side. Thomakin had chosen Attacus as his Centurion, for he was an ex-gladiator who had survived many combats and the other men regarded him as a bit of a celebrity.

"I'm not entirely happy, Thomakin," Attacus announced as they marched along.

"I be sorry to hear that. I want all my team to be motivated and content. Is there anything I can do?"

"You promised me I would be your Centurion. But with only fifty soldiers, I'm only a half- centurion. You've tricked me."

"Well, surely half a century is better than none?"

"That's not the point, Thomakin. A promise is a promise, and I have my career to think about."

"Don't fret, Attacus. Our little troop is only the start. We'll be recruiting from all our new allies, and each of them will send us some soldiers. So pretty soon you'll have your whole century, although I believe that officially there be only 80 soldiers per Centurion. In fact, not only will you be a full Centurion, but pretty soon we'll have a whole cohort, and after that a complete legion. And remember, you be my top military man, first in line for a generalship when we need one."

"Oh, goody! I can't wait." Attacus drew himself up to his full height. "And you will find no more loyal, no more valiant, no more courageous solder in battle than me, I assure you."

"Well, we will try to avoid battles, if we can. Think of yourself more a source of peace for our subjects."

Attacus was non-committal. Frankly, he was of the opinion that his new boss was perhaps a little naïve. No one becomes a great leader without breaking a few heads, and he, Attacus, was just the boy to break them.

But the ex-gladiator's dreams of acclaim in battle were soon put on hold, and instead he found himself and his men facing the mundane tasks of military life. For while Tiberius and Thomakin had arranged to house the army in the outhouses of the villa, this could only ever be a temporary arrangement. The soldiers were instructed to pull out the shovels and picks they had been issued with and set to work constructing the first Roman style camp in Britain.

The day after their arrival, when Tiberius announced that he and Thomakin were going later to negotiate with the head man of the local village, Lustia pouted. "You're not leaving me here, are you?"

"Daughter, we are going on man's work. We have a task to carry out, and the best place to start is with Bosman. He has been dealing with me for years now, and he's done very well out of it, I have to say. If we can't persuade him to throw in his lot with Thomakin, we have little chance with anyone else."

"And why do you think that this is a task only for you boys?" Lustia sneered.

"You are a married lady now, with a household to look after. Attend to your own tasks, daughter, and Thomakin and I will attend to ours. Is that not right, Thomakin?"

"Well if Lustia wants to come along, I see no harm in it," the new husband replied.

"Son-in-law, you will need to take your woman in hand. Otherwise she will completely control you."

"I don't mind being controlled, as long as she's happy." Thomakin answered, at the same time placing a gentle kiss on his spouse's forehead.

Tiberius walked off, shaking his head and muttering "Young love. What's the world coming to? I despair."

"You'll have to forgive Daddy. He's a bit old fashioned, but he means well. And you will see, there are always times when a woman's wiles can make all the difference in difficult political situations."

She had that glint in her eye and Thomakin wondered if perhaps his father-in-law was right after all. But what was done, was done, and he didn't want to disappoint her.

And so it was that the three of them, accompanied by one of the slaves leading a donkey, turned up later that day at Bosman's village. They were greeted with acclamation and expectation. Tiberius always brought goodies from Rome when he returned from these trips.

"Tiberius, my friend, did you have good time in Rome?" the village leader said, with one eye on the panier strapped to the back of the donkey.

"I did indeed, Bik. And I have brought back some gifts for you."

Bik Bosman bowed low in a deferential bow that was as insincere as it was ostentatious. "But you shouldn't have, Tibs. You are such a kind, generous person. Sometimes, you are really too good to me."

"Perhaps I am, but I really do appreciate your friendship."

"Freely given, Tibs, freely given." Now that Bik had been assured of his booty, he could turn his attention to the rest of the party. "And you've come with your beautiful daughter, too. But who is this gentleman with her?"

"Bik, meet my new son-in-law, Thomakin. A young man of considerable talent and excellent prospects."

Thomakin, delighted to be able to return to his native language, greeted him. "I be happy to make your acquaintance, Mr Bosman."

The fluency of Thomakin's Celtic tongue took the village leader aback. "But, you're not Roman, are you? You're a Briton."

"Indeed he is, Bik, and an exceptional one too. But more of that later. Come and see your presents."

The slave removed the panier from the donkey and spread its contents on the ground. Bik Bosman's eyes lit up. There were beakers and plates. There were beads, brooches and belts, all sparkling in gaudy colours, and the headman lifted them in the air and began handing them out to the clamouring peasants, keeping the most attractive items for himself, of course. Thomakin was now sufficiently knowledgeable in his role as a merchant to see that what had been passed over was no more than a load of cheap rubbish to be acquired in the Roman street markets for a few denarii for the lot. But he could also see that Bik Bosman did not know that.

Once the gift-giving ceremony was over, and the happy villagers had carried their share of Roman munificence back to their huts, Bik called on his wife and daughters to bring refreshment for their guests. They all sat on the ground while a downtrodden woman and her two eldest teenage girls placed food and drink before them.

"Skivvi, take yourself and the girls back to the house, where you belong. We have men's work to discuss." Thomakin saw Lustia raise her eyebrows at this dismissal of her fellow females, but fortunately she said nothing.

Perhaps the lady would like to take a walk around the village while we men get down to serious business," Bik suggested.

There was a hint of a nod from Tiberius, but Thomakin grasped his father-in-law's arm before it flowered into a full-on expression of agreement. "Mr Bosman, when you have travelled as I have, you will know that not all customs are as yours, and our ladies be encouraged to take an interest in their husband's affairs. With your kind permission, Lustia will remain and listen attentively to our discussions."

There was a firmness in Thomakin's tone of voice that caused the British chieftain to pause before answering. "As you wish," he replied eventually, "but it wouldn't happen with my women."

Tiberius rushed to begin their intended discussions before his daughter had time to react to such blatant misogyny. "We have a plan, Bik which will add considerably to your wealth, not to mention your standing in all the neighbouring territories. If you join us in our venture, greatness awaits you."

"Yes indeed, sir. You would soon be The Great Bik Bosman," Thomakin added.

"Sounds good. Go on, Tibs."

"Our project is to unite all the tribes of this island under the benevolent leadership of Thomakin here. As I have already indicated, he is a young man of exceptional qualities, trained and experienced in both military and business leadership. Under his guidance, you cannot fail to prosper."

Bik sneered. "He looks a bit skinny to me to be much good at fighting."

"Mr Bosman, I am happy to demonstrate my skills. If you have a great champion in your village, call him here and we will do battle, him and I. To the death, if you so wish. But I urger you to consider carefully, for it would be a pity to lose your best fighter so easily."

"Well, Tibs, I cannot deny your boy here is a brave one, and cocky as well. And he may be as good as you say, but all the same this alliance cannot be."

"And why is that, Bik? You are turning down fame and fortune. With Thomakin in charge, and with my contacts with Rome, you will see your trade boom and you will be protected from the avaricious ambitions of the Roman senators."

"The outcome is indeed attractive, Tibs, but the conditions are unacceptable. I am my own man, and nobody gives me orders, especially a young whippersnapper like him, no matter how brave and cocky he may be. Now if I were to be the one to lead all Britain, then…."

"It cannot be, Bik. You are a worthy chap, and you're doing a good job in this little village, but the leadership of all Britain is beyond your abilities. Only Thomakin has the vision and abilities to achieve what we seek."

"Well, I will have to stay poor then."

Lustia, who had been following all this carefully, coughed loudly to attract the attention of the men. "Mr Bosman, I think you are right. All this business talk is a little boring for a lady's ears. Maybe I should go and ask your wife to show me around your beautiful home."

Bik laughed loudly and slapped his thigh. "Now that's more like appropriate behaviour for a woman. And I'm sure Skivvi will be delighted to display our accommodation to you. It is well furnished, thanks to the kindness your father has shown my village. And my little Skivvi keeps it so nice, too. Do you know the way to my dwelling?"

"Yes, thank you, for I saw your wife enter it a few minutes ago. If you will excuse me, gentlemen." So saying, she left them to their discussions.

An hour later, when Lustia came back from visiting the Bosman household, the men were still in the throes of their negotiations. Tiberius and Thomakin were earnestly trying to convince Bik of the benefits he would accrue from joining their alliance, but Bik was still stubbornly insisting on his independence.

"How's the men's work going?" she asked, a self-satisfied smile playing at the corner of her lips.

"We're making progress, but still have the finer details to sort out," her father claimed.

"Maybe you should take a break and come back in a couple of days.," she suggested, and then carried on before they could answer. "Your home is beautiful and so well organised, Mr Bosman, and I have learned much that will be helpful to me, as a new wife. Skivvi has been so kind in showing me round and explaining things, and I would like to return the compliment, with your agreement, of course. So I have invited your wife and eldest daughter to visit our villa tomorrow, where I will do my best to introduce her to some Roman cooking and household activities which I feel can only enhance your lifestyles. It is an opportunity not to be missed."

Skivvi, who had accompanied Lustia from her hovel, nodded enthusiastically. "Yes Bik, I'd love to go, for I have never seen a Roman villa and Lustia has been telling me about many interesting things which will me make a better wife for you."

"Woman's things, I suppose. Well I see no harm in it, wife. As long as you make me a nice dinner before you go."

"As always, Bik. And the other girls will serve you with all the attention you deserve."

"Then it's agreed," Lustia said. "I will send someone to bring you tomorrow around noon. Goodbye for now."

Friendly farewells were exchanged and the visitors set off for their villa. As they were walking along, Lustia quietly took her husband to one side.

"How did your deliberations really go?" she asked.

"A little disappointing, my love. Bik remains to be persuaded that the benefits we offer are worth sacrificing a little autonomy for."

Lustia patted his arm and her voice was overflowing with reassurance. "Do not worry, my dearest one. Everything is in hand."

22 MEETING THE NEIGHBOURS

Eleganta Bosman was looking forward to what she hoped would be the most exciting day in her life so far. Although some might think she had done well in marrying the village chieftain, it was not the zenith of her ambitions. Bik was a fine enough man, if a bit stupid, but he was too easily satisfied. He didn't care about the size of the pond as long as he was the biggest fish in it. Sure, she had the best house in the village, but there was the trouble. It was a village house, just like all the others, although perhaps better furnished. But her visit to the opulence she anticipated she would find in Lustia's Roman villa would be her path to luxury. She was sure of it.

She just wasn't appreciated; that was the problem. Bik had demeaned her by giving her that stupid nickname, and though the village wives were respectful to her face, she could feel them pitying her behind her back. None of the men in the settlement had any time for their woman, but in this matter Bik outdid them all. He hadn't even deigned to give his daughters names, calling them 'first daughter', 'second daughter' and 'third daughter'. To Bik, no one else mattered but Top, the only boy. She loved Top too, but didn't the girls have a right to a future as well? Today, with Lustia's help, she would secure one for each of them.

The promised party arrived to collect to collect her and her daughter. It consisted of two men in tunics and metal helmets with spears and shields, and a third dressed identically but with a sword at his side and no spear or shield. The last of these addressed Eleganta, or Skivvi, as she was known to him. "Missus Bosman, we've been sent to escort you and your daughter safely to the home of the lady Lustia.

"Are you gentlemen bodyguards, or something?" Skivvi asked.

"Yes. Sort of, missus," the leader of the party answered. "My name is Attacus. Will you come with us?"

"Lead on, sir. My daughter and I put ourselves in your hands."

As they walked, the daughter carefully positioned herself beside Attacus, and quickly took great care to stumble on a convenient twig, so that Attacus was obliged to grab her arm. She speedily entrapped it in a tight grip. "Thank you for saving me, Mr Attacus. Perhaps I should hold on to you as we walk, in case another accident should befall me, if that's all right."

"It will be my pleasure," he answered.

"Oh, goody. My name is Bella, by the way. But, I say, those are strange clothes you and your friends are wearing. But you're not Roman, are you? You're a Briton."

"My team and I are all adventurous Britons who had strayed to Rome, but Tiberius and Thomakin have brought us back to help them unify the country. I myself am an ex-gladiator."

The pride in his voice proved impervious to the young Bella. "What's a gladiator," she asked.

He looked down at her. "Well it's some one who fights professionally. In the arena. To the death, sometimes."

"Oh, I say, you must be very brave. I think you should give up that gladiator stuff, all the same. Much too dangerous. I mean to say, I've just met you, and I wouldn't want to lose you too quickly." And, as Bella said this, she gripped his arm even more tightly.

This exchange between her daughter and their fierce looking escort did not go unnoticed to Skivvi. Of course, marrying her daughter off was part of her plans, but it needed to be to the right man. This Attacus seemed a bit too rough and ready; not the sort of chap she had in mind at all. She would be having a quiet word about him with Lustia.

They arrived at the villa with Bella firmly glued to Attacus, to be met by the waiting Lustia. "Thank you, Attacus," she said, "you may leave your charges here. Off you go now and continue building the camp for your soldiers, but in no circumstance must you come back here until I send someone for you. The villa is reserved for us girls this afternoon, and no man, including my father and husband, may enter until we say so." Attacus and his two henchman bowed formally and withdrew, leaving the ladies alone. "Come on in, Skivvi, I have prepared a real treat for you and your daughter."

"Thank you, lady Lustia, but could you please not call me 'Skivvy'. It is just a nickname given to me by my boorish husband. My name is Eleganta."

This seemed to surprise Lustia. "Eleganta, how very Roman?"

"It was given to me by mother, who has always insisted that my father was a passing Roman merchant."

"My, oh my, we could be sisters then. For I know my father was not always meticulous in adhering to his wedding vows."

"I would be very proud to have a Roman sister, Lustia. But if I do, it is unlikely to be you, for your father would only be a child when I came into the world."

"Well, never mind. We can be sisters in spirit, then. What do you think of the house?"

They were in the atrium, and the two Britons were as overwhelmed as Thomakin had been when he first saw it. "It is so beautiful, and this water thing is just…delightful." Eleganta said. As for her daughter, Bella's eyes were as wide as her mouth and she was struck dumb by the sight of such opulence.

Lustia noted with satisfaction that the sense of envy she had been expecting had manifested itself. She swept her arms all around the room. "You know, you could have this as well. And more, as you will see. For I have arranged for you to experience Roman baths before we enjoy the best of Roman cuisine. Follow me."

As the party passed through the various spaces on the way to the baths complex, the eyes of the two guests widened and widened. Eleganta was astounded by the beauty and the opulence of Lustia's home, and she could see from her daughter's face that she too was impressed.

"We're all girls here, so throw of your clothes and get into the water," Lustia said as they approached the baths. And to encourage them, she divested herself of her robes and climbed into the pool in the tepidarium. Eleganta and Bella looked at each other, shrugged, and stepped out of their grubby tunics and into the water to join them. Lustia escorted them through the same procedure as Tiberius had done for Thomakin when he had first arrived at the villa, until the two guests found themselves face-down on marble benches while their bodies were oiled in sweet smelling scents and pummelled by sturdy female slaves.

Eleganta expressed her pleasure with a sigh. "I feel so fresh and invigorated. So clean. It seems a pity to put our smelly tunics back on now."

"No question of that," Lustia answered. "We always dress in fresh garments after a bath." She clapped her hands and a couple of slaves appeared with their arms filled with white dresses. They handed one each to the two guests. "Gifts for you, please put them on and we shall go to dine and to chat."

There was a sumptuous feast waiting for them, and as they lay on the benches of the triclinium enjoying the culinary pleasures Lustia had so carefully arranged for, the serious chat began.

"Oh," said young Bella, "if only I could live like this every day."

"But you can," Lustia replied, "and you will. You both will, if you help me in my plan. Do you want to hear it?"

"Oh please, please," squealed Bella. Eleganta was somewhat more cautious in her response, but there was nothing to be lost by listening.

"My husband has a great destiny. It is to unite all the tribes of your land under his guidance. You will all be better protected from your enemies, and, working together with us, you can trade more effectively with others. We will all become rich, and luxuries such as I have here will be available to all, or at least to all the leaders of the communities."

"Do you mean that Bik and I could have a villa like this?" Eleganta asked.

"Indeed you may. In fact, if all goes well, you may even have this very one."

"But where would you go?"

"Thomakin will be the King of Britain, and I his Queen, in the fashion of the great Greeks in times gone by. A great palace will be built, and I will live there surrounded by my chosen 'great ladies'. Servants and slaves will look after us. The ladies will be the most important in society, much sought after by the sons of rich and powerful families, and will all make excellent marriages. And I wish you, Bella, to be my first and most important lady companion."

Eleganta could hardly believe her ears. She could see a utopian vision of all she wished for materialising in front of her. Living in this great house; the lifestyle she felt she was entitled to; the respect of the common people rather than their pity; the very best husbands for her daughters. She was being promised all her dreams.

"There is but one impediment. I am afraid your husband Bik is standing in the way of all of us fulfilling our hopes and desires. He does not wish to join with us in our venture. Girls.. ladies.. we must overcome this obstacle."

"But why ever not? What does he have to lose?"

"He is a stubborn man, Bik Bosman, and set in his ways. He fails to see what the future has to offer him. My husband's plan was to unite groups of villages into bigger units and appoint a Lord over each region. Your husband was to be the first of such appointments. But it seems his ambition and vision does not extend beyond your little village. He is obsessed by autonomy, and refuses to cooperate. If he does not take this opportunity, not only for himself, but for his son, another will do so, and you will all be forgotten while others rush to riches and glory. You must make him see sense."

"But how are we to do that? As you said, my husband is stubborn and bossy, and what power do I have over him to make him change his mind?"

"Even the most intransigent of men can be manipulated. Have you heard the story of the old Greek play by Aristophanes, Lysistrata?"

"No we never get that kind of entertainment here," Eleganta replied.

"Then let me tell you about it…" Lustia began, in a conspiratorial whisper.

23 REVOLTING WIVES

Attacus and his men escorted the two British women back to their village, where the first thing Eleganta did was to go round the houses rounding up the village wives for a meeting. When they were all gathered around her, she began her plea. "Our men are depriving us of our rights, keeping us poor and downtrodden. And, I'm ashamed to say, my husband, and your chieftain, Bik, is the main culprit. But life does not need to be like this, and we can change it." And she went on to explain the plot of Lysistrata and the plan Lustia had outlined to her.

Then, holding aloft a small amphora, she announced, "In this container is our secret weapon. It is called Aphrodite's Secret What you have to do is this. Go home and collect your best and cleanest garments. Take them down to the river, where you must bathe until you are fresh and spotless. Then put on the clean dresses and tunics you have brought. After that comes the coup-de-grace. Splash copious quantities of the secret weapon over your face and neck. Only then will you be prepared for the struggle that lies ahead."

The ladies ran off, all excited to sample the 'secret weapon' and to improve their lot, for what member of the female sex is ever satisfied with what they have? Bella and Eleganta made their way back to their own, now seemingly dingy, little hut.

"Powerful stuff, that Aphrodite's Secrete. Drives men mad," Eleganta said to her daughter,

"I know, Mumsy. It was all I could do to keep Attacus's hands off me on the way back today."

Eleganta frowned. "You are paying too much attention to that man. He is a mere soldier, a nothing. I have higher hopes for you."

"But Mumsy, he's not just an ordinary soldier. He is a half-Centurion, soon to become a full one. He is Thomakin's right-hand man in military affairs, and is destined to become a great general. And he's very cute."

"Well he may be a young man with prospects, but he's still a soldier. Don't get too fond of him or you'll be sorry; he'll probably come to a very young and extremely sticky end."

Bella hung her head and said nothing. Luckily, her mother could not hear the insistent beating of a lovestruck heart.

When they reached their house, Bella saw her father was out, somewhere. As head of the village, he considered himself an administrator, which as far as she could see, meant doing not very much. Administration was apparently the art of telling others to do those things you couldn't be bothered doing yourself. She supposed he had probably gone to join some of his cronies for an afternoon drinking session. But it was just possible that some urgent and unavoidable crisis had manifested itself and required his attention, but, if not, one was coming later, once her mum's plan went into action.

But there must have been a cog missing from her mother's machinations, because Eleganta told one of the younger sisters to go and find the village Druid. When the girl brought him back, her mother took him to one side and whispered something in his ear. Bella couldn't hear what it was, but the Druid kept nodding attentively and intermittently muttering comments like *I understand, I won't forget*, and *you can rely on me*. When he left, Eleganta's self satisfied smile indicated she was well pleased with the outcome of her little tete-a-tete.

While the family were wating for father to come home, the mother daubed herself from time to time with another dose of 'Aphrodite's Secret.' So much so that the room acquired a nauseous air, and Bella wondered if her mum had gone too far.

Dad arrived home eventually, a little tipsy. He had obviously been out for pleasure rather than business. When he saw his wife, he began to leer. "You look gorgeous, my little one. And you smell so sweet too. You've put me right in the mood for a bit of loving."

"Then you're out of luck, Bik. For I am most displeased with you."

"You mean, you're denying me my conjugal rights?" he slurred.

"Yes I am, until you fulfil your marital obligations to act in the best interests of your wife and family. Tiberius gave you a fantastic offer that would have improved all our lives, and the lives of the rest of the village as well, and you turned it down, because of your stupid pride."

'Oh, oh', Bella thought, 'my dad won't stand for that.'

She was right. He drew himself up to his full height, and without tottering too much, bellowed. "Keep out of things that don't concern you, woman. And take those fancy clothes off. Stick on a dirty old smock and go and roll in the mud. I want my old Skivvi back."

"She's never coming back. And from now on you call me by my proper name, Eleganta."

This was too much for an inebriated Bik. Emitting a scream of anger, he began to cross the floor of the hut, menacing fists raised, but his three daughters interposed themselves between him and their mother.

"Woman, enough of your insolence. Submit to your master's desires!" Bik bellowed.

"It shall never be. And let me tell you, it's something I'm not going to miss much."

Enraged, Bosman surged forward but found his path blocked. Bella had grabbed a knife from the kitchen and she now held it aloft. "Leave her alone! You're drunk. Go and lie in the corner and sleep it off. Or, so help me, I'll use this."

Bik paused, weighing up the situation. Bella knew he had always been a bit wary of 'first daughter'. He had never showed her any affection, so he could hardly expect filial love and respect. And she had often shown him he would never be getting it. She knew he would take that waving knife pretty seriously.

Bik froze where he stood, but his anger hadn't subsided, but had merely been tempered by a bit of fear. He continued his tirade. "Tell that woman it's time she knew her place. I make all the decisions here, not her. No one tells me what to do."

"You stupid old fool, the whole village is against you for keeping this great opportunity from us," Eleganta shouted back.

"Rubbish, woman. You don't understand anything. The lads in the village are totally loyal to me. They were just telling me so this afternoon."

Before he could say any more, he was interrupted by a loud commotion outside the door. Bella shouted to the boy Top to go and see what as going on..

Top came back looking a shade or two whiter than when he had left. "Dad, there are a load of your lads outside demanding to talk to you. They're waving swords and screaming and they say if you don't come out and sort 'this' they'll come in here and carry you out. Whatever 'this' is."

"Oh, what now? Right, you lot. I'll be back, and we'll get this all sorted. And I mean you too, Skivvi."

"Eleganta," she shouted after him as he was passing through the door.

When Bik returned half-an-hour later he was a different man. For a start, he was sober. And he was plainly wounded, although there was no blood, or broken bones. Bella guessed that the wives of the village had stuck to the plan outlined to them by her mother, and the husbands hadn't liked it. It was her guess that her father had been given an ultimatum that he couldn't refuse.

This guess was confirmed when she heard Bik muttering. "What a shower of weaklings! Can't even stand up to their women." It struck Bella that he was conveniently forgetting about his own current domestic situation.

"Why don't you go and have a word with the Druid? He always knows what to do in difficult situations," Eleganta suggested.

Bik ignored her, but a few moments later he rose and announced he was going to see the Druid, as if the idea had just come to him.

As soon as her father had gone, Bella ran to her mother. "Mummy, what will the Druid say to Dad?" she asked.

"How would I know such a thing?" Eleganta answered,

"Come on Mumsy, I saw you talking to him."

"He will tell your Dad that he could not just surrender to our wishes, or he would lose face and power in the village. But if he could squeeze some extra benefits from Thomakin and Tiberius, he could claim he had been holding out for a better deal, his reputation would be enhanced. And the rest of us would get what we want. Win-win all round, I would say."

Bella was impressed by her mother's cleverness. She could see that she herself would need to be even smarter if she was to keep hold of her Attacus against Eleganta's wishes.

24 THE PLAN COMES TOGETHER

One of the ancillary pieces of information that we gleaned from the Stones was that the British custom of 'Elevenses' has a longer tradition than you might have imagined, as we saw when we translated the section below. When I read it over to my colleague, I mentioned that it gave me the notion for a cup of tea myself, and Joanie jumped up immediately and made me one. Ah, the joys of co-habitation! But to our tale...

Attacus was having his usual mid-morning refreshment in his tent when one of his men approached, dragging a young British adolescent by the ear. "Centurion, I caught this piece of trash trying to sneak into the villa."

The centurion waved his hand to indicate the soldier should leave the boy there while he downed the last of his wine. Then he leaned back on his camp stool to luxuriate in the warm glow. Finally, when he was ready, he addressed the youth. "Well, sonny boy, what have you been up to."

"I've a message from my mother to the lady Lustia," the lad answered, a hint of defiance in his voice.

"Do you now? And who might you be? And what does your mother have to do with my Lady Lustia?"

"I be Top Bosman, the son of the village chief, and my mother be Eleganta, also known as Skivvi."

"What is this message, then?"

"Ah, you can't catch me out like that, mister soldier. I have strict offers from Mum not to divulge the message to anyone but the Lady Lustia herself."

"Have you now. Well..." Attacus lay back in his stool again, his face adopting an air of rumination intended to indicate that he was considering the options. The defiant Top remained unfazed.

Eventually the centurion spoke up. "So you're Eleganta's son...Bella's brother then?"

"Indeed I am, soldier, and from the top family hereabouts, and we don't expect to be messed about by the likes of you."

"Mind your manners, young man. I'm in charge here, and you'd do well to remember that. I'll tell you what, though. If you do something for me, I'll take you to our Lady."

"What is it?"

Attacus rose from his stool to rummage in a chest at the back of his tent. He emerged carrying a rather large and ornate brooch. "All you have to do is give this to your sister, and say it comes from the valiant Attacus, an ardent admirer of her beauty."

Top, being still of the age where relations between men and women are considered gross, gagged visibly. But he was smart beyond his years, and never missed an opportunity. "What else will you give me?"

The centurion's response was to draw his sword and wave it around in an exceedingly menacing but competent manner. He executed some rather impressive moves around the boy's head. Top didn't flinch. "I'll teach you to fight like this, son," Attacus announced.

Top smiled. "Agreed, take me to the Lady."

The pair of them set off for the villa, Attacus expounding on the theory of 'gladiating' and Top listening in admiration. They were now the best of pals.

When they were shown into Lustia's presence, Top ran up and whispered his message in her ear. Her immediate response was to call for her father and her husband. While they were waiting, Attacus murmured to Top out of the side of his mouth, "And don't forget to give my message to Bella."

The men of the villa appeared and Lustia barked out her commands. "Dad and Thomakin, prepare yourselves, for we must return to the village to see Bik Bosman. I can assure you that our venture will succeed if you only follow my remaining instructions."

Father Tiberius swelled out his chest and furnished himself with a stern expression of disapproval, as might be expected of a man in the face of a pushy woman going beyond her remit. But Thomakin interrupted him before he could begin to scold.

"What have we to do, dearest one?" he asked his wife.

"You must be diplomatic, darling. I can assure you that Bik is now disposed to accept your offer; in fact, he is obliged to do so. But you must not make an enemy of him, we will need him as a loyal subject."

Thomakin smiled with contentment at being allied to such a smart lady, and even Tiberius seemed impressed.

Lustia continued. "So here's what you have to do. When we arrive in the village, you will tell Bik that you have been considering his thoughts on the matter. Perhaps he did not fully understand what you were offering. At the moment he is head of the village, a prestigious and worthy position. But our plan, ours AND his, will mean so much more. Obviously, King Thomakin cannot control a country made of hundreds of small villages. They will be organised into groups, which we will call baronies. At the head of each group will be a Lord, running the whole barony on behalf of the King. You tell Bik you have chosen him as the Lord of this region, and he will be the First Lord and indeed the most important to you. So he will not be giving up power by joining us; he will be increasing his power."

When he heard this, Thomakin put his arm around Lustia. "Smart girl, my wife. Don't you think so, Father Tiberius?"

"Hmmph," her father replied, a tad grudgingly. "Let us get on now and sort this out."

The Stones, in no great detail, confirmed that Bik proved to be delighted with the unrefusable offer from Thomakin and accepted it with alacrity. In the months that followed, Tiberius took King Thomakin and Queen Lustia, together with the Lord Bik and the Lady Eleganta, to all the villages in the region. Nor did the process of negotiating with the village leaders prove to be as difficult as it had been with Bik. The Stones only provide one example of such negotiations, adding that, as the encounters always followed the same path, to outline them all would be superfluous.

The negotiations would begin with Tiberius introducing the village leader to his companions and explaining that he had come to offer them access to untold riches and other delights. Delights which went far beyond those they had already experienced in their previous dealings with him - him a trusted merchant who always delivered on what he promised. At this point, the Ladies Lustia and Eleganta would excuse themselves, saying that they would like to acquaint the village women with some of the new delights which would be available to them. The village councils of the region were uncomfortable discussing serious political matters in the presence of the female gender, and always agreed to this request, little suspecting they were contributing to their own downfall. Lustia and Innocenta would leave, clutching an amphora of Aphrodite's Secret.

The men would continue humming and hawing over the proposals without making much progress, until Lustia and Innocenta reappeared in the company of the wives, concubines and girlfriends of the men of the council. These ladies would position themselves very close to their appropriate men, would wink and smile, and tell their partners to accept the offer, whatever it was. The men, intoxicated by their sweet smelling ladies and overcome with lust to such an extent that their reason deserted them, would round on the chief and insist on the proposals being accepted. The chief, no less under the influence of Aphrodite's Secret than his councillors, would stretch out his hand towards Thomakin, saying only one word. "Deal!"

Thus it was that in each village, a few adventurous young men would be added to Attacus's cohorts, and some local girls would be incorporated into the royal household. In a matter of three months, the previously unheard of Pre-Roman Barony of Wessex was established, with Lord Bik and Lady Innocenta at his head. Now, the Stones tell us, the new King Thomakin was able to leave the whole region in capable hands and move on to organising and annexing other areas of Britain.

25 THE TROUBLESOME PRIEST

The landscape of Southern Britain in the time of Thomakin was not what it is today. The Romans had yet to invade our sacred lands and spoil it all with their incessant road building. A process, incidentally, which has been assiduously pursued ever since: just look at the spider's web of tarmac that has completely destroyed our rural ambience. Nor had the forests been decimated to build the great armadas that permitted us to dominate the high seas. Agriculture had not, so far, gone mad, polluting the countryside with hedges and 'No Trespassing' signs. Avaricious limited liability companies had yet to scar the fair earth in their greedy search for underground treasure which would ultimately destroy the very air we breathe. In Pre-Roman Britain, nature was as nature had intended itself to be.

The Stones describe this arcadian paradise in some detail, with its majestic trees, lush greenery and deep blue lakes. It speaks of a warm day in early summer when, beside one of these watery havens, in a clearing in the forest masked from prying eyes by great, protective oaks. The sweet, intoxicating scent of Aphrodite's Revenge wafted in the air. Two lithe young bodies lay, entwined together, recovering from the exertions brought on by their passion. One of them was the young Lady Bella, lady-in-waiting to Lustia, the Queen of all the Britons. The other was the recently nominated General Attacus, officer-in-chief of the fast growing army of the King Thomakin. Silence reigned over the scene, as the couple wallowed in the warm glow of post-coital satisfaction.

The stillness was broken by Attacus saying, after a sigh which might possibly have indicated contentment, "I am not satisfied, dearest Bella."

"Do you want to go again? Was it not good for you, my love?"

"No. no, dear. It was perfect. YOU are perfect. I am talking about other matters; about the situation with my life and career."

"But, my godlike one, you have just been appointed General and OC of all the British forces. What more can you wish for? You now have two squadrons under your command. One to stay here and protect the barony, under the command of your disciple and my brother Top. And the other for you to lead to glory as The King and Queen go forth throughout the land and unite all the British people in one great Kingdom."

"You may not understand this, but I am, you see, a soldier, a fighter, an ex-gladiator. Combat runs in my blood, and if I don't get it, well, my life is incomplete. And while the King, aided and abetted by the wiles of his lady Queen, have achieved miracles in uniting the whole of Wessex with no blood being shed, I fear he may be able to do so everywhere. And what would be the point of me then, dearest one?"

"Fear not, Attacus, for the Queen has taken me into her confidence and we have discussed this matter at length. Thomakin is a kind and affable man, and it is true that he is hopeful of achieving his goals without violence ever being necessary, but the Queen is doubtful that such a hope can be realised. Evil people are everywhere, and they are devious and unscrupulous. Through their machinations, they have achieved positions of power, which they use for their own ends and not for the good of the people they are supposed to protect. It is therefore to be expected that they will reject the utopian image King Thomakin will lay before them, and your military powers and your army will be called into action. Glory and acclamation await you, my love, so be not disheartened."

"I am glad to hear this, my angel, and I do hope our lady Queen is right."

"But one word of warning, Attacus. If… no… *when* you are called into battle, be careful. For I am very fortunate to have found you, and I do not wish to lose you now."

"Have no fear, my little one. For I will be relying on my great prowess in the arena, and on the ring of protection of your undying love. I am invincible. But duty calls. We have had our pleasures today. Let us get dressed and go, for if my soldiers are indeed to go into action, I must continue with their training. And the Queen may be in need of your help and counsel."

The two young people, somewhat reluctantly, re-robed and walked off, hand in hand, into the trees, leaving the idyllic clearing in its silent natural splendour.

It was not left in its quiet isolation for long. For, as soon as the lovers had disappeared into the trees, a dark hooded figure emerged from behind a sturdy oak tree, where he had been concealed, listening to the couple's secrets. There was no doubt as to who this was. It was the village Druid, a man whose demeaner and character fitted exactly the evil people Bella had described a few moments earlier. Through his wiles, he had inveigled himself into the confidence of the Baron Bik, and his malicious ambitions were only held in check by the even more wily Lady Eleganta.

His mind was racing with wicked schemes and roguish stratagems. And there, alone in the forest, safe from prying ears and eyes, he aired them at full voice. "Here is my opportunity," he rasped. "For this plan of that Roman lacky, Thomakin, will not sit well with the high priests of my order. His successes to date will only inflame them, for it is they, the servants of the gods, who must rule all our lands. This usurper will be subjected to the deadly Curse of the Druids, and a bad end is assured for him. And I, a lowly priest at present, can be the instrument of his downfall. I will run now to the High Council, and tell them all that I have seen and heard today. They will surely reward me, and I too will be one of the great chosen ones once we have divested ourselves of this unholy traitor and restored order where it belongs, in the hands of the chosen instruments of the gods."

And in his turn, the Druid left the clearing, but in the opposite direction to the young lovers. As he disappeared behind the trees, his loud cackle betrayed his wicked dreams of wealth and power.

Just as I had feared, my Joanie reacted badly when I read this latest episode of our history to her. Indignation was too polite a word for her reaction 'Charlatan,' she shouted, preceding it with a word I cannot bring myself to write here. She then launched into her habitual diatribe against those superstitious fraudsters who invoke their gods to perpetuate evil deeds and issued her standard warning: if any one of them touches a hair of the head of my Thomakin, I'll do for him, see if don't. In vain I pointed out that we were talking about ancient history here, that Thomakin was in no way 'hers' and that the hairs of his head had long ago turned to dust. This did not satisfy her, and she stormed out saying she was going for a walk to clear her head, leaving me wondering if she would be back in time to make dinner.

26 THE RIVAL

I have to confess to having some difficulty in ensuring that I am recounting this history in the strict chronological sequence in which the events took place. As I mentioned earlier, the dating system information on the Stones remains undecipherable, and each Stone contains more or less a complete chapter in the story. When Joanie and I found them, they were scattered in a seemingly random manner around the site, with no semblance of order. My problem is exacerbated by the fact that there are two threads to the story: that of Thomakin Kobbler's adventures and the record of events back in Beaufox Headman's village from which Thomakin had been banished.

The sequence of events as I present them is therefore my own, constructed as best as I could from the context of the writings. While I am confident my conclusions about timing are quite correct, I feel I need to make this problem known to you, in the interest of historical accuracy.

I am pretty certain that what happened in the section below does follow on sometime after the establishment of the Wessex Barony described immediately above. I contend also that these events in Beaufox's village must have occurred before the cataclysmic happenings which you will read about later. But history is about interpretation, and as a reader you are, of course, free to draw your own conclusions.

One of the effects of Beaufox Headman's union with Innocenta Kobbler was that his standing and reputation as leader of his village improved. He was no longer hated and detested; he was merely intensely disliked. Time was a factor in this, as recollections of the legendary Thomakin faded from the memories of his friends and relatives. But the main reason for this marginal improvement in Beaufox's reputation was the control his consort had over the worst excesses of his character.

"I have no problem with violence and oppression in search of our goals," she said to him one day. "But vindictive violence and oppression is something I just cannot tolerate." At this point Beaufox opened his mouth to defend himself, but Innocenta raised her hand to silence him. "And don't tell me we need to show them who is boss. They understand full well who the boss is. You, and, through you, me. The needless imposition of power is counterproductive, Beaufox. In times of trouble, we will need all the villagers on our side."

Suitably chastised, the village chief hung his head. "Yes, dear," he mumbled. But inside he was seething with rage. It was only his intense love for her that kept him from inflicting some gratuitous violence on her. Instead he walked out and assuaged his anger on two of the village dogs. (*When the Stones revealed this behaviour to us, it prompted a tirade of righteous indignation from my Joanie.*)

The Stones also provide another explanation for the grudging acceptance by the villagers of the Beaufox-Innocenta rule. Being a lady of outstanding intelligence, and coming as she did from a solid working-class background, Innocenta had identified many instances of inefficient working practices in the way the village's iron-age economy was functioning, and used her power to change them for the better. As a result, the village became richer, and while most of the new riches were directed towards the ruling family, it was inevitable that some of the benefits would accrue to the ordinary villagers. Finding themselves better off than before, they began to think that, just maybe, Beaufox and his wife weren't such bad apples after all. *(If only modern regimes could avail themselves of such detailed practical knowledge, what a better place the world would be. A vain hope, I'm afraid.)*

At this point you may be thinking that Beaufox and Innocenta weren't a bad thing for the village, (and, ultimately, mankind) but alas, you are too ready to forget their flaws. You will remember that they were two evil and ruthless individuals, and their greed was boundless. So when a passing trader arrived one day and let slip that there was a young Briton with a powerful army in the process of uniting all of the lands under his control, Innocenta Headman realised that here was an opportunity that they had missed, and summonsed the travelling merchant to dine with them, with a view to grilling him for more information.

"What exactly is this so-called King actually up to?" Innocenta asked the visitor.

The trader gave his version of Thomakin's progress in the arduous task of taking over the country. As he understood it, villages all over the land were flocking to his standard. All those whom he visited were agreeing to his terms, and those whom he hadn't yet visited were sending delegations begging to be allowed to join. It was hard work, but the would-be King was on the way to success.

"But what does he get out of it?" Beaufox asked, for the idea of anyone expending effort without receiving personal gain was alien to him.

"Hah! What to you think? Money! Wealth! Riches! For the man is a charlatan, nothing but a lackey of those Roman merchants who are coming over here and destroying our indigenous trade. He is insisting his subjects sign exclusive deals with the Roman trader, Tiberius, who just happens to be his father-in-law. Soon there won't be an indigenous merchant left in our land. Bloody foreigners!"

"And what is the 'King' called?, asked Innocenta, for his name had not yet been mentioned.

"King Thomakin. Some even call him King Thomakin the Great."

Both sets of hosts' ears pricked up at this revelation of the name. Could it be…? But no, it could not be possible.

The guest went on. "Although he is married to a Roman, it is said that he is a Briton. Apparently he was banished from his village as a result of a subterfuge carried out by some despotic village chief, and he fell in with the Roman merchant during his travels. The rogue Tiberius took him to Rome and married him off to his daughter."

Beaufox's mouth fell open, but Innocenta dug him in the ribs. Turning to their guest, she smiled sweetly. "How interesting? Well, well, well, it's getting late. May I thank you for your visit and your illuminating conversation? I will call one of our servants to show you to your bed, where I hope you will have a comfortable sleep before going on your way tomorrow. Good night."

As soon as the visitor had been despatched, Innocenta turned to her husband. "Bit of a shock, that."

Beaufox was raging. "That bloody Druid, Cathbad. I told him to execute the rat, Kobbler, not send him out in to the wide world to continue to cause havoc. I'll have his guts for this."

"Calm down, husband. It never makes sense to act in anger. Let's take this calmly and rationally. It seems to me there are two things you must do."

"I'm listing, my little bunny."

"First of all, our villagers must never get to know what our Thomakin is up to. Otherwise all those Kobblers and Armours will rush off to find him, bring him back here in triumph, and it'll be curtains for us."

"So, what to do?"

"Call your henchmen. Get them to escort that merchant out of the village, making sure he doesn't talk to anyone.

Then, when he's a safe distance way, tell them to bump him off."

"It shall be done, my dear. And what was the second thing?"

"Anything Thomakin Kobbler can do, we can do better. After tomorrow, we start our campaign to take over the other villages and submit them to our rule. For I have long thought that your ambition was not up to your ruthlessness, and you were too ready to settle for the mediocre and a happy life. So gird up your loins; greatness awaits us and together we will achieve it."

Beaufox always did his wife's bidding, so the next day the British trader's peregrination of the British terrain was brought to a sudden, violent and permanent halt. And soon after that, the Armours were called into action, pumped full of propaganda about the god- given destiny of their tribe. They were fed false rumours that an invasion was taking place, led by a wicked and cunning Roman who was pretending to be a Briton, although his wife and his whole family were Romans. Thus armed with righteous indignation and nationalist fervour, they were sent out to conquer the local area.

As I read my translation of this part of the history out, I assumed that Joanie would burst out in indignation again. I was totally wrong. Instead she sat there with a broad smile on her face. My quizzical look must have prompted her to speak.

"The fools! The stupid fools! That's it then. My Thomakin and his faithful friends will ensure that those two evil schemers get their just desserts. I am wallowing in the warm glow of justified retribution. Fancy a cup of tea?"

27 THE DRUID COUNCIL

Beaufox's plans to increase his power went very well... at first. But then, the nearby villages headed up by his close relatives were the low-hanging fruit of his territorial expansion. His uncles, cousins and second cousins were not exactly enamoured by the idea of handing over control to another member of the family, especially not Beaufox. For one thing, they had never forgiven him for marrying out of the family. And for another, they were all familiar with the rumours surrounding the sudden and unexpected demise of his father and elder brother that had led to his elevation to chieftain. But it was exactly those rumours that rendered them reluctantly acquiescent to Beaufox's demands. None of them wanted to end somewhere in the depths of the forest being devoured by avaricious wild boars.

But when Beaufox moved on to the other surrounding villages where he had no family connections, things got a lot tougher. The kinder ones listened to his proposals before rejecting them out of hand; the others, in the majority, just laughed in his face. The latter response always raised his blood pressure to astronomical limits, and he would have drawn his sword and disposed of the respondent there and then, had not Innocenta pulled him away and whispered quietly in his ear, "Not this way, dearest. Be patient."

Back in their own luxurious roundhouse, they sat down to review progress. We're never going to manage this, Innocenta," Beaufox moaned.

"Don't be a big softy, dearest. What did you expect?"

"Well, Thomakin apparently didn't have this problem? Look how well he's doing"

"Thomakin's a notoriously nice guy, everyone likes him. That is not an advantage you have, my sweet one. But instead, you have ME. So listen now. Things are not so bad. We've got all your family on board, with their militia to add to our own resources. Gather these fighting men together and paint them up with copious layers of woad. Then march them down to one of those recalcitrant settlements and put on a show of force. That should frighten those troublesome leaders into submission."

"And if it doesn't?"

"Well, we'll just bump the guy off and put one of your sickly cousins in his place."

The Stones record that Beaufox had some success with this stratagem, although progress was slow and the amount of territory he acquired was somewhat limited. By contrast, according to the Stones, Thomakin made rapid progress without ever having to resort to shows of strength, and soon had the greatest part of the island under his control. It could only be a matter of time before he found his way into the Beaufox fiefdom.

The news of Thomakin's advances continued to reach the Headmans, through the mouths of the traders who frequently visited the settlement. Many of those knew nothing of the rising King's origins. They were allowed to depart in peace. But any who showed signs of having information that would have allowed the identification of King Thomakin were handed over to the axe of Beaufox's henchman, Nobrane Hunter.

Eventually Innocenta decided that the threat was too imminent to be disregard any longer, and convened a council of war, at which only she and her husband were present. They had too many evil secrets to share their thoughts with anyone else.

"We need a plan, husband," she said to Beaufox, "for at this rate the dreaded Thomakin will turn up at the gates of the village before we're ready for him."

"Agreed," her husband replied, and waited. He had long ago accepted that her ideas were always better than his.

"This is a tricky problem," she told him. "First of all, while you have done well in reinforcing the Armours of the village with men from our subject settlements, it is still the case that Thomakin's forces vastly outnumber ours. Moreover, he was always the best fighter in the village when he was here, and the rumours are that he has a general who has won plaudits as a Roman gladiator. And, of course, if he turns up here at the head of his army, our boys will see who he really us and desert us to join his ranks. So defeating him in battle is not an option."

"It would appear so, my sweet one."

"Therefore, much as it pains me to admit this, it appears that we will have to make some sort of deal with him."

"But why would he deal with us? As soon as he walks in here, the whole village will be on his side. What reason would he have to negotiate anything with us?"

"You are right, husband. We must secure this deal *before* he enters the village. *Before* any of our subjects see him and figures out who he is. But I have a solution."

"You always do, my love. That is the most attractive thing about you."

"Stop flattering and listen! We will send out a delegation led by your trusted servant, Nobrane Hunter, to meet him, and to offer peace talks in a neutral location. Somewhere close to the boundaries of our territory where we have at least some control."

"Why would he accept?"

"Nobrane will emphasize that it is to avoid bloodshed. Thomakin is a merciful man, dedicated to the cause of peace. He will agree."

"What a brilliant wheeze, my sweet one. Only you could come up with such a thing." He leaned over and kissed her.

She allowed him this indulgence, but only for a few moments, before she pushed him off. "Now, where can we meet him?" she asked.

"Where? Where? Let us think."

While they were contemplating the options for a suitable location, the druid Cathbad rushed in to interrupt them.

"Get out," Beaufox snarled. "We are in secret conference here, and YOU are not invited."

Cathbad would normally have withdrawn immediately when so addressed, for he was frightened of Beaufox. But there must have been someone else who terrified him even more, for he stayed and mumbled, "But.. but...there are some people here who want to speak to you."

"Tell them to make an appointment with the guard at the door, like everyone else. Now, leave us in peace!"

While Cathbad was bowing low and trying to stammer out a reply, the visiting party strode into the hut, uninvited. They were dressed in what was unmistakably priestly garb, but not the sort of priestly attire that Beaufox had ever encountered in the village priests. These men were beasts of a higher order. Their high hats almost brushed the ceiling of the dwelling, and their jewelled staffs sparkled even in the dim light inside the building. Their long cloaks were embroidered in many colours, and the decoration was enframed in ritual shapes sewn in gold and silver thread. Their clothes and their demeaner spoke of one thing – their importance- and it was a message screamed loudly to all who beheld them.

"Beaufox Headman, we must have words with you," the one who appeared to be the leader barked, tapping his staff on the ground to emphasise the message.

"I'm busy," said Beaufort, for, whoever they were, they were in his place, not theirs, and the familiar surroundings gave him an unjustified sense of confidence.

This proved not to be an acceptable answer. The leader raised his staff above his head, and waving it around in a ceremonial manner, he intoned, "The Curse of the Druids be upon you for your insolence. May your offspring be tiny and malformed, and your dynasty short-lived." As the head druid spoke, flashes of lightning emanated from the end of his staff, missing the bewildered Beaufox by inches. "Are you ready to listen now?"

Beaufox gulped and nodded.

The Druid went on. "We, the Great Council, are displeased with you. For you were meant to dispose of the rebel Thomakin Kobbler, and you messed it up. Now he is wandering at will around our lands, turning the people against their own true gods and their chosen representatives in the land of the living."

"We were going to deal with him," Beaufox muttered, without much conviction.

"In your own inimitable incompetent manner, no doubt."

Beaufox was about to protest at this slight, but Innocenta grasped his arm and shook her head. It was obvious to her who wielded the real power here, and it wasn't her husband. "We are preparing to summon Kobbler into our presence, and when he get hold of him, we will deal with him."

"Are you now? Now, that might be quite useful," the head Druid said. "But we cannot trust you to handle this to our satisfaction. I will tell you exactly what you will do with him, and I will assign two of my high priests to supervise you and make sure you do the job right. Pay close attention, for I shall now describe the plan to you."

At this point, the Stones did not go into the detail of the plan, and I must say I felt a touch of trepidation for the young Thomakin. To my surprise, Joanie did not share my fears. "Poor Thomakin," she told me, "for he is so good and innocent he could be very vulnerable. But all will be well, for luckily he has the worldly-wise Lustia looking out for him.

As an aside to the story, I should point out here that as I translated, I felt some nervousness at the Stones' mention of the lightning flashes from the Head Druid's staff. To the unscrupulous false historian and conspiracy theorist, it is an opening for them to suggest that the story of the Stone's was not history, but legend. This would be an inaccurate deduction. For a start, there is the corroboration of the story provided by the Livy text in Rome, which I have already mentioned. There is also a very simple scientific explanation for the phenomenon of the lightning from the staff. Static Electricity!!! So, to further silence any potential critics, I can reveal that the Department of Archaeology at Reading University, a very respected organisation in the field, has been provided with drawing of the druid staff, and a team of experimental archaeologists are at this very moment constructing a replica, and preparing a demonstration of how manual manipulation of the item can produce the apparent magical result of a terrifying release of an electric charge

28 THE FAMILY REUNION

The Stones tell us that the location chosen for the meeting between Beaufox and Thomakin was both exotic and atmospheric. Imagine, if you can, walking through a deep forest, tall trees hiding the sun and only an occasional ghostly streak of light penetrating their leaves and branches. In the gloom, you stumble through the undergrowth, tearing your clothing and scratching your arms on the thorny bushes that border your path. From time to time, your feet sink into soft moss or squelch through glutinous mud. You lose your balance often, and fall over many times. Progress is slow and difficult, and you feel your temper rise as you battle against the difficult terrain. Such was the progress of Thomakin and his entourage as they made their way to the appointed place.

Continuing on your imaginary journey, you walk out of the trees into a scene that seems from another world. A narrow band of green grass leads to what appears to be a large lake. The mist hanging a few inches above the water obscures everything beyond the bank, and yellow sunlight diffuses through its opaqueness. Barely discernible, in the water at the edge of the lake, a small boat, something like a coracle, floats. Inside the boat, a wizened old man in a long grey cloak sits, holding an oar aloft and gazing towards the forest. Such was the sight that greeted Attacus and his band of soldiers, when he emerged from the tress at the head of King Thomakin's expeditionary force. He thought for a moment that he had died, and here was the ferryman waiting to take him to the lands of the ancestors.

"Oi," shouted the man in the boat, "You be the King Thomakin party on your way to meet my master, Lord Beaufox?"

"We be," Attacus replied. "The King is just behind us."

"Well, I be here to row you over to the island."

"In that thing? You won't get us all in that flimsy little vessel."

"I can take three, that be plenty to conduct the talks with my master."

Just at that point Thomakin and the rest of the party emerged from the forest. "What's the problem, Attacus?"

"This fellow has been sent to take us over to see Beaufox in his little craft, but he can only take three passengers."

"Not a problem. You and I and one of the soldiers can go," the ever acquiescent Thomakin said.

Attacus shook his head. "No sir, I cannot allow it. I must go with two of the men and check that it is safe, and that no skulduggery is going on. Then I'll give you all the all clear, and you can come over with another couple of the legionaries."

"As you wish, Attacus, but be careful."

Attacus climbed into the boat with two of his men, and the little ferry set off. They watched it go, but it soon disappeared from sight in the mist.

When they could no longer see the coracle, Lustia turned to her husband. "I will be going with you, so there will only be room for one soldier on the next trip. And no arguments, for you know I am indispensable when it comes to negotiations."

This was unchallengeable logic, so Thomakin said nothing.

From time to time, the voice of Attacus boomed clearly across the water and through the mist. "All well so far."

The boat eventually arrived at an island as densely forested and as mysterious as the mainland.

"You go that way, sir," the ferryman said, pointing to a path leading into the trees."

"All well, we have landed. I will call you if it's safe. Can you hear me?" Attacus shouted, before moving off.

"Hearing you loud and clear," the voice came back from the mainland.

Satisfied, Attacus drew his sword and set off into the trees, followed by his two legionaries. They had only gone a few yards into the forest, when a host of wild savages, their faces exotically painted in blue, descended on them. A fierce battle ensued.

Attacus and his two men fought valiantly, slaying a large number of their assailants, and would have certainly carried off the day, had it not been for the unfortunate incident with the sword and the stone. It happened thus: Attacus was dealing with one particularly vehement savage, and swung his sword with such violence that he hacked off one of his attackers arms. Unfortunately, the momentum of the weapon carried it on until it cleaved a large rock beneath the painted amputee and stuck there firmly. Attacus struggled bravely to free it, but without success. He was so distracted by the effort that a horde of half a dozen screaming savages were able to fall upon him and cut him into little pieces. The other two members of his party, discouraged by the fate of their leader, turned and flew. But they only managed a few yards before they too were decimated by unfriendly axes.

One of the victorious Britons, probably the leader for he showed more commercial acumen than the others, must have worked out that the Roman sword would make a fetching trophy for his hut wall, and that it may even have had some intrinsic value were he to sell it. He began tugging valiantly at the sword, but without success. It was lodged solidly in the rock. He gave a shrug, and muttered, "It'll be a long time before the man to pull that thing out comes along."

So saying, he walked to the edge of the trees and gave a thumbs up sign to the waiting ferryman, who made his way to the edge of the water, and, looking back across the lake, bellowed, in a voice undistinguishable from that of the newly deceased Attacus, "All well here! No danger!. Am sending the little boat over to collect you." And he jumped into the coracle and began rowing.

When the boatman brought Thomakin, Lustia and their bodyguard back to the island, Beaufox and Innocenta were there to greet them, with a guard of honour perhaps excessively equipped with ceremonial weapons.

"So we meet again, Kobbler," Beaufox said, his cunning grin illuminating his face.

Thomakin stepped out of the boat and gave a little nod, but Lustia was having none of this insolence. "My husband's name is **King** Thomakin. And he is to be addressed as 'Your Highness'.

Beaufox visibly gagged, but he was prevented from an outburst of anger by a sharp dig in the side from Innocenta's elbow. Instead, he settled for a frosty glare.

Thomakin, as ever affable, merely nodded his head again and said "Headman." No handshakes were offered on either side.

Innocenta chirped up. "My husband's name is **Lord** Beaufox, but you may address him as 'My Lord'."

That was too much even for Thomakin, who stared defiantly at his old adversary.

"That's right, Innocenta. You tell him, dearest," Beaufox said.

The name of Beaufox's wife caused Thomakin to pause for reflection, and stare fixedly at the young lady. "Innocenta…Innocenta… Not a common name. Almost unique, in fact. I only know one Innocenta, and you be indeed the right age to be she. And I be sure I detect a family resemblance. Tell me, be you indeed my little cousin, Innocenta Kobbler?"

"Kobbler as was, Cousin Thomakin, but I am now Lady Innocenta Headman."

"But, did he force you, little one? Did he thrust his unwanted attentions on you? If indeed he did, I will wreak a terrible Kobbler revenge on the scoundrel." As he said this, he placed his hand on the hilt of his sword.

"Stay, Cousin, for I can assure you that my darling Beaufox has always treated me with deference and respect, and indeed even defended me against the prejudices of his own family."

"But, little one, you have allied yourself to… to this man. Do you not know of his invidious character, his history, how his devious machinations led to my downfall?"

"My husband has been much maligned, Cousin, and his probity and integrity has never been properly acknowledged."

"So you've gone over to the dark side, then?"

"Thomakin, Beaufox has explained to me that what happened to you was the result of a very unfortunate mix-up. You should put it aside, let bygones be bygones and concentrate on the future. For we are on the verge of something momentous. We have the opportunity to make Britain great, let us not throw away this chance."

"Hmmph!" Thomakin grunted, but he did not dissent.

Beaufox raised an arm and pointed into the forest. "It's this way, if you would please follow me and Innocenta," he said.

The two couples, each arm in arm, ambled regally along the indicated path, which was in the opposite direction from where the three hacked-about bodies of King Thomakin's advance party lay in pools of blood under the trees They were followed by the guard of honour, and then by the King's now sole bodyguard, sword drawn, ready to pounce at the slightest sign of trouble.

29 THE TRIAL

Hidden deep in the forest, the edifice, to which Beaufort led his guests was a revelation to them. For it was not a mud hut topped with straw for a roof, like those used everywhere by the tribes of Britons. Indeed not, it was something else entirely. *This great stone building with its intricate decorations is described in great detail in the hieroglyphics of the Stones, accompanied by very graphic illustrations. Undoubtedly, a full description of this previously unknown type of ancient building will be released to the general public once the academic study of the stones that I have instigated is complete. There will no doubt be news items on all the great TV channels, and several enthusiastic and earnest young students will almost certainly take up its study and receive well merited Doctorates of Philosophy for their efforts. But for the purposes of this work, and in the interests of progressing the history of the events, I will confine myself at present to an account of Thomakin and Lustia's reaction to it.*

"Wow! Some place!" Thomas remarked.

"Not unlike our own villa, but somewhat larger and more luxurious. Look at those magnificent statues of wild animals and people. And the furniture, look at the gold and jewels on those chairs," Lustia added.

"Quite a home you have here, Beaufox," Thomakin admitted.

"It's not mine. I live somewhat more modestly. It belongs to a friend."

"He must be some kind of god to have a place like this."

"Something like that," Beaufox said, quickly, " But come. A sumptuous repast has been prepared for you. While we eat, we can work out the details of our cooperation."

The whole party repaired to a room that resembled a traditional Roman triclinium, where a long table overflowing with fruits, sweetmeats, and other delicacies was surrounded by highly ornamented sofas. Around stood several young lads, scantily dressed in what seemed like their underwear, and carrying silver trays. On seeing them,

Lustia whispered to Thomakin, "These boys remind me a bit of our Vestal Virgins. Wrong gender, though."

"Settle yourselves on the sofas and get your teeth into what's on offer. No one can ever say Beaufox isn't a good host," Beaufox said, waving a ceremonial arm over the victuals. Then he grabbed an apple and took a huge bite. "Go on, go on," he encouraged his guests.

One of the boy servants lifted a plate of fruit and offered them to Thomakin, who chose what appeared to be an appetising apple. He was in the process of lifting it to his mouth when Lustia grabbed his arm and stopped him.

"Soldier," she shouted. The bodyguard who was accompanying them came up to her side. "Taste!" she ordered.

The soldier took Thomakin's apple from his hand, and Lustia watched as he bit, chewed and swallowed it. When he hadn't collapsed after a few seconds, she turned to her husband. "It seems OK. You can eat the rest." The soldier handed the remains of the apple to his king.

"Don't you trust me?" Beaufox asked.

Lustia shook her head. "Not at all, You've got form. Thomakin's told me all about you."

The meal proceeded in the same manner, with the bodyguard pre-tasting everything that Thomakin and Lustia ate or drank. This procedure was a bit of a conversation stopper, and it wasn't until they had finished eating that they got down to the nub of the matter.

"What exactly are you offering us?" Innocenta asked, and Beaufox nodded in appreciation of his wife's political skills.

"You'll be made a baron of the whole district, with all the rights that come with that," Lustia replied.

"This district is already under my control. You're offering us nothing," Innocenta answered.

Thomakin leaned forward and eyed her and her husband in a very regal and authoritative manner. "Headman, if you don't join with me, you'll be on your own. You'll be an a enemy of every other Briton, and you'll have no friends or any protection in times of trouble.

"Don't listen to him, Beaufox," Innocenta whispered, "the gods are on our side."

Lustia laughed when she heard this. "The gods? Your gods, you mean. Do you think your British gods are more powerful than the Roman gods by whose benign will we Romans have conquered almost all the whole known world? Your gods are as nothing compared to ours. Am I not right, husband?"

Thomakin nodded his agreement. "She's got a point, Beaufox. When you look at the facts, the Druids' gods be pretty insipid compared to the Roman deities. And we have the Roman gods on our side. Time for you to change allegiances, I would say. Chuck out the Druid priests and turn to the true religion."

Beaufox had no time to formulate an answer, for the booming of a loud drum rang out, followed by a fanfare of trumpets. A long ceremonial procession entered the room. At its head, a tall bearded figure dressed in a highly decorated hooded cloak. From beneath the hood, two piercing blue eyes shone out from a wizened face. As he walked, the staff the figure carried beat out a slow march, and the staffs of his companions, following in pairs behind him, tapped in unison.

When he arrived right in front of a bemused Thomakin, the Hight Priest stopped, and his deep voice bellowed an incantation. "I have heard enough! Treachery is revealed. The Curse has been actuated. Secure him, minions!"

Two of the acolytes grabbed Thomakin and thrust him to the floor at the feet of the Druid leader. They placed their feet on his back and pressed down so hard that he could hardly breathe, never mind move.

"Well done Beaufox. Your task is over, you may dispose. Take your woman with you," the High Priest commanded.

Beaufox and Lustia retired backwards, bowing and genuflecting, until they disappeared through the open door.

"Let the novitiates clear away the victuals and the trial may commence." The young lads who had served the meal quickly cleared the table and disappeared.

"Who will prosecute the case? A forest of willing hands were raised. "You, Cathbad, may have the honour, for you have served us well in this matter." Beaufox's pet Druid bowed and smiled to himself.

"And who will speak for the defence" All priestly eyes descended to the floor and all priestly feet shuffled uncomfortably. "Come on, someone has to do it."

Each of the group visibly shrunk in stature as they tried to avoid drawing attention to themselves. An irritated Head Priest pointed a finger at random. "You, you are the defender. It is, I know, an onerous duty, but due process must be observed. Let the trial begin. Cathbad?"

Cathbad spoke up. "It's an open and shut case, your worship. You yourself heard the accused denigrate our gods and attempt to usurp them with his Roman pretenders. I call for the ultimate penalty."

"Sentencing later," The Head Priest reminded him. "What defence does the accused offer?"

The unfortunate priest designated to defend Thomakin coughed apologetically. "He did it, your worship. It is an undeniable fact."

"Well, of course he did. We all heard him. But are there any mitigating circumstances to be taken into consideration? Is he of sound mind, for example?"

The defending priest reached down and, grabbing Thomakin by the hair, lifted his head from the floor. "Are you a bit do-lally?" he asked Thomakin. Thomakin raised his eyes and opened his mouth to speak, but the priest pushed his head to the floor again before he had a chance to do so. "Perfectly sane," the priest told his boss.

"In that case, it's the ultimate sanction. Let him be sacrificed to the gods. Take him away, lads."

At this point a horrified Lustia throw herself on top of her husband, and began to wave her arms around frantically. "You beasts. You horrible beasts. This cannot stand. You cannot separate me from my husband. I will never abandon my Thomakin. His fate is my fate."

"Just as you like," the High Priest said. "Take her as well, boys."

The unfortunate pair were dragged feet first from the building and taken to a clearing in the forest, where a large bonfire had been prepared. The cohort of priests, led by their chief, paraded around it, waving their staffs and uttering incomprehensible incantations. When they had finished, the Head Priest raised his staff aloft, and chanted the dedication. "Oh ye gods, we offer these traitors, these unbelievers, as a punishment for them and as a gift for your delectation. Take them with our gratitude for your protection and wisdom."

As he finished this ritual, the bonfire was set alight. "Throw them on, lads and let's get this over with and get back to the monastery. It's dinner time already and I'm getting a little peckish."

Thomakin and Lustia were thrown into the fire. The flames immediately engulfed them, and as their bodies burned, the Roman hopes for a peaceful submission of the land of the Britons went up in smoke.

30 THE CURSE OF THE DRUIDS

I'll always blame myself for not realising how much the untimely end of Thomakin and Lustia had affected my Joanie. My only excuse is that I was blinded by the historical significance of the tale that the Stones had revealed to us. I'm afraid I let myself effuse over my analysis of the facts. "Just think, Joanie," I almost shouted, "if Thomakin and Lustia had survived, what could they have achieved? They could have built a strong country; one which no foreign power would dare to interfere with. They may even have gone on to found the first great Northern European empire, to rival - nay, even to surpass - those of the Romans and the Ottomans. But history tells us what actually happened. Obviously Beaufox was no Thomakin, and the whole great unification scheme fell apart. Then someone brought word to Caesar in Gaul - maybe it was a furious Tiberius - of the failure of his great venture. Old Julius hot-footed it over here to teach the

British a lesson, and would have done so too, if more urgent matters had not recalled him to Rome. But less than a century later, the Romans came back and made us a vassal state. Of course, we were still a disorganised shamble of disparate tribes, so we were easy meat. Nor did we get it together in time to prevent those Germans and Scandinavians, and then the French, helped themselves to our lands. But to think of how it could have been: we could have had a Kobbler dynasty that endured for centuries. Britons could still be ruling their own nation, instead of a mixed bunch of foreigners."

At the time, it seemed strange to me that Joanie didn't share my enthusiasm. She just sat there, with her long face and sad, sad eyes. But, to my shame, I failed to see the signs, and carried blindly on. "What a historical breakthrough we have achieved. We've made it, Joanie. We'll be like Howard Carter and Lord what's-his-name, or that Edinburgh woman that found the last resting place of Richard the Third. Academic recognition will be ours. They might even give us our own programme on Discovery Channel or Sky History. Once I find a publisher for our account of the Stone's story, we'll be famous."

It was only when Joanie didn't react to this prospect of celebrity that I realised something was wrong. Her sad eyes had by now transitioned into steely cold weapons of anger. "Something not right, dearest?" I asked.

"The bastards! The Druid bastards! How could they do such a thing to MY Thomakin and his beautiful and clever wife. May the fires of hell descend on them all!"

I remarked that this was a strange remark for an atheist to make, but Joanie was in full-flow and ignored me.

"May they be damned to eternal misery. May their every day be filled with pain and remorse. May they suffer from a sore back and toothache for the rest of their existence."

"Those sentiments seem a little out of place given your religious views, my dear. And besides, their existence was over two millennia ago."

She must have heard at least the last part of that comment, because she said, "Well, if not them, their descendants."

"I'm afraid all that's left of the Druids is a few weird hippie types who smoke dope and eat tofu."

"Not just them. All those irrational superstitious weirdos who gather in fancy buildings and seek advice from intangible beings from another universe. It's high time they were banished to the sticks, and all their influence over the ordinary people destroyed. Wipe them all off the face of the earth, I say. Let logic reign."

I was beginning to get alarmed at her vehemence, and made a vain attempt to calm her down. "Joanie," I said in the firmest voice I could muster, "Joanie. Remember the Curse of the Druids. Now I'm as much an agnostic as you are, but what if the believers are right after all. Why don't you temper your language a little bit. Just in case. No sense in tempting fate, eh?"

My suggestion had the opposite effect from what I had intended. I should have realised it hadn't worked when Joanie paused to draw breath to such an extent that her ample breasts expanded by two bra sizes. Then, suitably armed with sufficient supplies of air, she exploded. "NEVER!!! THEIR INFLUENCE WILL BE DESTROYED FOR ETERNITY. IT SHALL BE AS IF THEY NEVER EXISTED."

And that's when everything went black.

Although it was a bright sunny afternoon outside, darkness descended inside the room as if a blackout curtain had been placed in the windows. We were left in pitch black. Even the dull red standby lights on the TV went out. And then there was the silence. Deafening. And the smell: a permeating odour of stale incense. It boded ill. Evil was creeping into our bones.

The only positive effect was that it shut Joanie up immediately.

We waited, both trembling. A small ball of white light appeared in the centre of the room. A loud whooshing noise was heard, quietly at first, but slowly louder and louder. The ball of white light expanded, revealing a misty haze that it seemed to contain within it. As the volume of the whooshing increased, the mist thinned out to reveal the shape of what appeared, from his long hooded cloak, to be a monk. The full splendour of this personage was at first obscured. But as the mist finally dispersed completely, the figure was revealed in its full glory as what must have been an important officiate of unspecified religious order.

The apparition stopped towards my Joanie, until she too was bathed in the ball of light that had brought him. By this time the noise had grown to its full volume, and I expected a knocking neighbour to appear at our door complaining of the noise. But no one came; perhaps only we could hear it. Joanie was cringing as the ghostly priest stared her down.

"You have invoked the Curse of the Druids," the voice from the figure's mouth croaked.

"See, I warned you Joanie," I said. It was a retort that is never helpful at any time, and especially not at this time.

The voice continued, croaking the curse that the stones recorded as having been uttered when poor old Thomakin was banished from his village. "Oh gods, oh spirits of the land and the rivers, bear witness to this Curse. If any person thwarts the will of the gods, disrespects the priests or plots against the chieftains, may he be condemned to a life of anguish, a horrible and painful death, and everlasting torment."

I remember thinking this didn't look too good. I would have tried to save her, to interpose myself between her and the apparition, but when I tried to move, nothing happened. Instead I had to stand there, helpless, and watch the proceedings as they unfolded before me.

The apparition pulled back his cloak to reveal what was either a short sword or a very long dagger, which he drew from his scabbard and waved aloft. It was a beautiful piece, worthy of pride of place in the British Museum, with a blade that shimmered in the light, and a golden handle encrusted in jewels. Probably worth a few bob if I could find one of those clandestine collectors to take it off my hands, I thought. I wondered if I would be lucky enough that he would leave it behind when he went. As it happened, he did, but not quite the way I wanted.

He raised the weapon and plunged it deep into the bosom of my beloved partner, screaming "Revenge!" Then he disappeared, taking his ball of white light with him. The darkness receded, revealing poor Joanie lying lifeless on the floor in a pool of blood, with the ceremonial weapon sticking out of her chest.

Looks like I'm making my own dinner tonight, I thought.

31 THE LAST WORD

I admit to being a little nervous as the man in front of me finished reading the last page of my manuscript. He lifted up his head to look at me. "So this is your story, then, Mr Phibba?"

I nodded.

He attached a document to the manuscript and pushed them across the table. "Would you mind signing here?" he asked.

"I looked over at my legal representative, sitting right next to me. She was shaking her head. I shrugged an apology.

"If you wouldn't mind, sir, I'd like a quick word with my client. Alone," my lawyer said.

"Of course. He lifted all the papers and walked to the door. The uniformed constable unlocked it and they both went out, locking it behind them again.

"I have to be honest, Mr Phibba, it's looking very bad for you," my lawyer went on.

"Why?"

"Your DNA was all over the body."

"Of course it was, I was trying to see if she was OK. She wasn't, as we now know."

"And the ceremonial dagger, bedecked in gold and jewels, that you claimed was used to kill her. It was a plain kitchen knife..."

"It had obviously been transformed after the event. As part of the Curse..."

"It was covered in your fingerprints, and no-one else's."

"Well, I took it out of her chest."

"Yes, you said that. But where were the fingerprints of the one who stuck it in there in the first place?"

"Do apparitions from the past have fingerprints?" I asked. "Look, I put a whole lot of work into researching this properly, I have all the evidence."

"Yes, well, on that point, those stones with the ancient writing on them that you sent to the museum. British Museum, wasn't it?"

"Yes."

"They say they never received them. Who were you dealing with there?"

"Doctor Foster."

"From Gloucester?" My lawyer grimaced.

"There you are then. That explains it. Foster has taken my stones with him to his new job in Gloucester Museum, to work on them secretly. He's obviously going to claim all the credit for my hard work, the charlatan."

"Hmmph! Well, there's also the matter of the Livy writings you found in Rome. At the Antiquity Centre, I believe you claimed."

"An admirable archive of Roman writing, if I may say so."

"It doesn't exist. There is no Antiquity Centre in Rome." There was a pause as my lawyers treated me to a triumphant grin.

"Oh no!! They've only gone and changed its name and moved it to another address. Who would have believed it?"

"Certainly not a jury, Mr Phibba."

"Look, I'm a professional historian. My mantra is truth at all costs. Of course they'll believe me."

"Mr Phibba, you're employed at the local library. As an assistant librarian support officer... under training. Your only qualification is one solitary GCSE."

"Well, it is in History."

" And it doesn't help your case that your friend Joanie inherited a large fortune the week before she was killed. And that you are the only inheritor."

"We were very close, Joanie and I. A couple, really. We were planning to get married. I miss her so much."

"Look, Mr Phibba, you're never going to win your case. My recommendation is that you change your plea and we plead diminished responsibility. I'm pretty sure the judge would accept that."

I looked at her, horrified at the very suggestion. It took me an age to control my indignation before I was able to speak. "No miss, I could never do that. Like I said, I'm a historian. For me, truth is everything."

END

Printed in Great Britain
by Amazon